Hearts Unravelled

Billionaire Romance Series (Book 3)

Lucy Appadoo

Dedication

This story is dedicated to all those who believe in love despite past wounds.

Contents

CHAPTER 1

Gina Cassani inhaled the warm breeze as she stood on brick-paved ground in front of an easel, dabbing a splash of purple on to her flower design, emulating the plants that grew up against her grey timber fence at home.

She flicked her shoulder-length auburn curls away from her face, and took a step back to scrutinise her painting. Her shed in the corner and flowers lining the perimeter. A bed of brush alongside the house with overhanging trees near her fence swayed in the breeze above a large patch of lawn.

Gina leaned against the outdoor table, pulled out the white steel chair, and sat with a relieved sigh. Painting was her escape from her role as a data scientist. It gave her a creative outlet beyond her usual factual projections and statistics, which she loved too, but painting took her to another place, another time. Where life had new possibilities and didn't drag her down as much as reality did. It was her safe place, where nothing could go wrong. It would truly be a dream come true if she could have her own gallery show one day, to display her deepest, darkest emotions made physical.

Gina relished painting landscapes, and abstract designs which expressed so much more than she ever could in words alone. Painting saved her from the darkness she sometimes held within, and she couldn't imagine not having her creative outlet.

The buzzing of her phone brought her out of her reverie, alerting her to the arrival of a visitor at her front door. It was her friend, Dalia.

Wiping her hands on her smock as she pulled it off, she quickly stepped inside, and thoroughly washed her hands before heading to the door.

She swung it open, her heart warming at the sight of her friend. "Hi, Dalia. You're early."

"Sorry. I can see you're in the middle of painting—I can keep myself busy while you finish." Dalia was impeccably dressed in loose-fitting pants and a tight, red top. Her lovely high cheekbones and copper-coloured hair matching her inner beauty. She pulled aside a wispy strand that fell down her cheek.

"No, it's all good. I've finished now. Come in." Gina led her to the two-seated white sofa with its plush, matching pillows. "Let me quickly get changed and I'll get you a coffee—or would you prefer a wine?"

"A wine would be great. Thanks."

Gina stepped inside her bedroom with its grey carpet underneath drawn curtains, a bedside lamp and a double bed with throw pillows. She changed into a black plain t-shirt and blue stretch jeans.

She returned to the living room holding two glasses of Merlot. "Here you go," she said.

"Thanks," said Dalia, whose chestnut eyes were fixed on her. She wrinkled her narrow nose. "Something's wrong. I can tell."

Gina sat beside her on the couch and sipped her wine, then set it gently on the glass coffee table. "I'm just worried about this new possible client we're seeing Monday. The pitch has to be perfect." She took a breath. "I've never worked for a chain of health centres before."

Dalia angled her head. "You shouldn't worry, Gina. It's the same job you're doing now but in a new industry. I'm sure you'll land the contract and learn the business in no time."

She nodded. "Even if I do get the job, what if I don't like the manager or staff? What if they don't see my work as helpful if they compare me to other data scientists, or marketers? Even meeting new people is daunting; you never know who you'll get. Am I going to clash? Will they like me, will I like them, and..."

Dalia held up a hand. "Stop right there, lady. You cannot focus on the future when you don't know if any of that will happen. Stop being negative and embrace the opportunity. You can learn so much in a new industry, and I have absolute faith in you."

Gina arched a brow. "But I don't know if I've even prepared enough. Sometimes it's like I let my painting get in the way as a distraction." She calmed her breathing. "It's hard to find a balance. As much as I'd like to sell my paintings, I don't have the time to market them. I always have this fear in my head that people will turn me away, that I'm not good enough, or I'll say the wrong thing."

Dalia sighed. "Don't make assumptions, beautiful lady. You need to make the time." She took a breath. "I'd be happy to go with you to meet a gallery owner."

Gina shrugged. "Maybe."

Dalia sat up straighter and clasped her hands together. "You know, if you were to start your own marketing firm, you could pick and choose your own jobs."

Gina nodded. "That's exactly why I want my own consulting company; for the flexibility and control over my work. It'd give me more time to work on my art too." She rubbed her hands together. "How is Luca, by the way?"

Dalia's eyes lit up, clearly still in love. "He's amazing. Two days ago he took me to see the opera, which I loved. Next weekend, he wants to take me to Daylesford for a hot spa day. Can't wait. It's never boring with him."

Gina beamed, part of her wishing she had that kind of love. "I'm glad he's treating you well after everything you went through."

Dalia drank down her wine as Gina's phone pinged with a message. "Who's that?"

Gina picked up her phone and clicked on the video chat. "Rose, how are you?"

Her other friend, Rose, lived in Tuscany with her gorgeous Italian boyfriend, living her dream life. "Ladies, so good to see you. I've missed you guys."

Dalia leaned forward and stared into the screen. Rose's kind hazel eyes and long, strawberry blonde hair accentuated her beauty. She also had a warm heart. "When are you coming back to visit?"

Rose sighed. "Hard to say, girl. The villa's been busy with more guests than I can handle. I might need to hire someone else. But I'm loving it. What's new with you two?"

Gina explained about her new client. "I always get nervous with potential new jobs and hope they take on board what I advise."

"I am sure you'll be fine, girl. Just take it one day at a time and you'll adapt quickly."

"I am so jealous of your gorgeous man, Gianni. Is he keeping you up most nights?" Dalia teased.

"Of course. I fall in love with him more each day. He's wanting to come to Melbourne in the next few months. We'll see. Now, I know how Luca is, Dalia, but what about you, Gina? How's your love life?"

Gina scoffed. "What love life? I prefer to be single."

Rose pointed a finger. "Listen to me. Do not let Steven turn you off men. Not all of them cheat."

Gina's chest ached as she closed her eyes briefly. "It was more than cheating, Rose. But please, I don't want to rehash it. We have enough negativity in the world without my ex coming into the mix."

"I'm sorry. I know it was hard, but I care, and we only want you to be happy. You're beautiful and deserve to find love too," said Rose.

"I second that," said Dalia, who inched forward and squeezed Gina's hand. "We love you and know you've got a lot to offer someone. It'll happen when you least expect it."

Gina remained silent, knowing she had stopped believing in love three years ago. Love couldn't be trusted when all it meant was pain. She might as well join a nunnery.

CHAPTER 2

Stephen drank a beer and sat opposite his friend, Dale, whose emerald-green eyes observed him while sipping on his bourbon. The brilliant, blue spring sky and rare billowing clouds brought in butterflies and other insects as Stephen took in the city view of South Yarra across from his balcony. Rustling trees and a warm breeze awarded him a stillness which he rarely took the time to experience, reminding him to divert his attention back to Dale. "I forgot to mention something." He exhaled. "You know that marketing company we might hire?"

Dale nodded as he placed a finger over his cleft chin. His shoulder-length black hair with its blonde highlights rippled in the breeze. "Sure. What about it?"

"On Monday they're sending over a data scientist who's going to assess our financials and discuss projections." Stephen was the CEO of *Katie's Health Group,* which was doing marginally well profit-wise, but had taken a big hit after a former health worker had committed fraud. It had harmed their reputation, and they had lost a few important clients. They needed to get back on track.

He downed his bourbon. "I heard she's a bit of a hard taskmaster, so you might have your hands full. But I also heard she's beautiful. Deadly combination, don't you think?"

Stephen waved his hand. "I'm staying away from women."

Dale laughed as he shifted in his timber-slatted chair. "Come on, man. You can't keep drinking your way to fun when you're thirty-five. Haven't you played the field long enough, my friend? It's time you put down some roots and settle down."

Stephen's heart clenched. "Just because you're married and have a baby doesn't mean I have to be. I'd rather focus on the business. Not to mention starting up the nightclub. I'll be busy, so why would I want to tie myself down? Besides, I've had enough pain in relationships to last a lifetime. I need my freedom." He couldn't imagine a baby living as he did in this inner-city house with its dynamic architectural design, and generous sized rooms he could use for guests and old friends. He'd have to child-proof the entire home. Besides, the idea of family made him sick to the stomach after he'd had those fantasies years ago.

He refused to go there. No, it was much better to be free while hosting parties and schmoozing new investors for future business. Being single was safe, and he could no longer consider trading his single life for a gut-wrenching relationship.

Dale shook his head. "No, that's your fear talking, Stephen. I know the pain you went through when you lost her, man, but you can't just let yourself grow old and lonely."

Stephen's chest constricted, but he ignored it and got up, heading to the couch inside. He pushed away his rampant thoughts. "Let's watch a bit of sport before I need to head into the nightclub."

His new business had started a few months ago, and he'd hired people he trusted. Stephen thoroughly vetted them to avoid being burned like he had with his last staff member. But his heart soared at how he thrived on keeping busy and being in charge of several businesses. With the guidance of his retired father, who had owned businesses all his life, he mastered the skill of investment and became a billionaire. But despite his wealth, he still had so much to achieve, like potentially building more nightclubs and increasing his art collection. He was a lover of art and keen to buy that perfect piece, which would honour his past.

The only problem was, he still hadn't found the one that spoke to him like a hit to the gut.

"I won't be able to make it to the nightclub tonight, Stephen, but enjoy it without me. I've got a family event."

"No problem. I've got to check the books and talk to the manager. I'm thinking of potentially doing karaoke or theme nights."

"So, you're wanting to draw in a range of demographics?"

"Yes and no, mainly focussing on the older crowd. They've got more money to spend than the younger ones."

"So true. Now, let's watch the game."

His phone buzzed on the glass table. Leaning forward, he picked it up and saw the display. The caller was his friend and communications consultant, who worked for him tirelessly and hardly took a day off. "Hey, George."

"Stephen, listen. That new firm we might use just asked for our numbers from several years ago and our last financial year's profit."

"Why now? Can't they wait until Monday?"

George laughed. "Apparently, the data scientist, Gina, said she wants to look it over now to prepare for Monday's meeting. She doesn't want to wait."

He exhaled, shaking his head. "My goodness. The woman is only pitching for us, but already giving us grief."

"Maybe, but if she can help us, it'll be worth it. Please get it done."

"On it, George. Enjoy your weekend."

He ended the call and turned to Dale, who glanced at him curiously, but Stephen put up a hand and switched on the TV to take his mind off his dreaded Monday. "Don't even ask." Had he made the right decision to consider this marketing firm, or should he look elsewhere?

CHAPTER 3

G ina stared in wonder at the smooth purple carpet that felt soft underneath her laced sandals, and the glossy round tables surrounded by high stools; wall-to-wall mosaic patterns creating a circular whirlpool, congested bar to the side, and dance floor filled to the brim. Deafening music assaulted her eardrums and young women singing aloud to the sound threatened to give her a headache. Why had she agreed to have a girls' night out with Dalia, who already had a boyfriend? She didn't need to be taken to a meat marketplace to wonder whether she'd find any men she could have a mature conversation with here—not that she was looking. Doubtful.

"Oh, wow. Look at all the neon lights. Can you believe how modern and upbeat this place looks? It's only a few months old; it's beautiful," said Dalia.

"Whatever you say," said Gina, glaring at a man eyeing her from head to toe. Why had she chosen this black satin dress with its high split and a low-cut neckline that fit so tightly it seemed to crush her lungs?

The nightclub's lighting was low and created an eerie atmosphere, which made it impossible to see anyone properly. Even the stage, which held a four-piece band playing jazz tunes, did little to perk her up. The music was too loud, the people too weird, and already her feet were killing her.

People pushed into her to pass through to the dance floor, so she shifted closer to the bar. "Let's get a drink, Dalia. What would you like?"

Dalia hovered at the bar and grinned at Gina. "I think the barman likes you. He can't take his eyes off you."

Gina shook her head. "No, he's looking at you, not me."

Dalia waved a hand dismissively. "Never mind. I'll have a vodka and lime. I'll get the next round."

Gina leaned over the bar and ordered their drinks. A Moscato for herself and a vodka and lime for Dalia. She swallowed at the smouldering gaze of the server, who was handsome enough but appeared to be in his early twenties—far too young. She wasn't here to meet anyone, anyway. More like doing a favour for her friend, who enjoyed nightclubs and men's intense gazes.

Dalia grabbed her drink. "Thanks, beautiful." She turned. "Why don't we head on upstairs? I'm curious to see what's up there."

"Lead the way," said Gina, who sipped her drink as they navigated the crowd.

Walking upstairs, she held on tightly to her glass, her bag over her shoulder, and holding on to the rail. Once they reached the top of the stairs, she rounded the corner until—*bam*—a heavy, robust chest knocked into her, causing her to gasp. Her drink spilled all over the top of her dress and the glass dropped out of her hands. "Oh, great. Thanks a lot." She winced at the chill of her drink against her chest.

"I am so sorry. I didn't see you there," said a man she refused to look at.

"That's obvious. How could you be so clumsy? I should send you my cleaning bill. Of all the...."

He tapped her elbow. "I really am sorry."

Gina looked up at him as Dalia dabbed at her chest with tissues, a smirk on her face, remaining silent as she observed the exchange.

Gina was speechless. *Hell!* The man looked like a high-end model from the front cover of a fashion magazine. His gorgeous looks deserved to be outlawed.

But she wouldn't get taken in by his unnervingly handsome features.

He wore tight, pleated pants, with ripped muscles protruding from his rolled-up white shirt, buttoned down to show a few hairs over a taut chest. His beard and moustache gave him a regal look, and his dirty-blonde crew cut and thick, pronounced eyebrows gave him the appearance of a bad-boy.

His looks wouldn't fool Gina, who could instantly tell he was a player. "You should be damn sorry. Now I'm drenched, thanks to you."

"I'll pay for the cleaning, and I will get you another drink."

She waved him away. "Oh, just forget it." Gina walked away without a backward glance.

Dalia leaned in next to her. "Are you mad? What the hell, Gina? Do you have eyes?"

"Yes, I do, but I won't get taken in by a guy who most likely thinks he's god's gift to women. God knows I've had enough of those. Too many immature men around in this lifetime and I'd be glad to remain a spinster my whole life rather than deal with these arrogant players."

Dalia huffed. "Oh, Gina. Come on. It looks as though there's another dance floor and bar here. A nightclub within a nightclub. Quite nifty. But let's get you cleaned up first."

"Let's go to the washroom. Then I'll get another drink and hope to never see that guy again for as long as I live."

Stephen had goosebumps. *Wow! Oh, wow!* Did his eyes deceive him, or was she the most beautiful woman in the world? That satin dress, which fit her body like a second skin, the curvature of her waist, the high split that showed a hint of smooth skin, and the low neckline which left little to the imagination. If she wasn't so rude, he would've asked to spend the night with her. No harm in a one-night stand with no strings, and the anger in those eyes was a turn-on. She was feisty and strong. But he also saw pain in her eyes.

He couldn't let her leave without buying her another drink. His head told him to stay away, but his heart drew him to her, despite her anger.

Decision made, Stephen turned back. If he explained he was the owner, she might be more understanding. It was for business only. He hated leaving patrons like that when she could easily leave a negative review. The club was still new, and he needed happy customers.

His eyes darting, he made his way back up the stairs. Pushing through crowds, dodging a drunken man, and ignoring ogling women, he forged on but couldn't find her anywhere. *Damn!* She had to have gone to the washroom, surely.

His manager, Lou, a broad-shouldered man in his twenties, approached him on his way to the bar and patted him on the shoulder. "Hey, man. Just wanted to give you a heads-up. That lady friend of yours is asking for you."

He sighed, shaking his head as he remembered their one-night stand after the opening of his club. Not only had he been drunk, but he couldn't remember her name. He had driven to her apartment but had left early morning. No doubt she'd have forgotten the sex, but she kept coming to the club and flirting as if they were in a relationship. What had he done? Why couldn't he resist beautiful women? He knew why.

CHAPTER 4

His legs weighed him down like lead as he sat by the bar opposite the bartender. "Hey, Bruno. Busy night?" Bruno's moustache and beady eyes made him look older than twenty-five.

"Of course, boss. You okay, man?"

"All good." He wasn't about to tell the man about his former conquest. He leaned over, careful to avoid the sloshing alcohol on the counter. "Any problems with patrons?" He caught a whiff of jasmine mixed in with lavender.

"None, man." Bruno dropped an umbrella into a mixed drink and handed it to a woman standing alongside him. Her hands were dainty, fingernails blood-red.

As he turned to the side, his chest exploded. The hot, sexy woman was back. "Thank you," she said.

Glaring in his direction, she walked back to her friend and whispered in her ear.

On wobbly legs, he made his way to the woman. "Please. Let me buy you a round. For...before."

She huffed. "No need. It's forgotten."

"Listen, I insist. This is my club, and I don't like having any patron leave my nightclub unhappy. I owe it to you."

She smirked. "*You* own this nightclub?" He nodded. "Good for you, and you don't owe me anything. Let's drop it."

Her friend gave her a strange look, then stepped towards him. "What's your name?"

He grinned, realising she was softer than the other. "I'm Stephen. And you are?"

She shook his hand. "Dalia, and this is my friend, Gina. She would gladly accept your drink. Thank you."

Gina drank down her wine making him jealous of the glass. "No, Dalia. It's fine. Please. Can we go now?"

"Come on, Gina. Have fun for once in your life. The man owns the club and is making a friendly gesture." She faced him. "This is an amazing place. How long's it been open?"

He swallowed and wished Gina would look at him. But instead, she avoided his eyes and stared into her hands. "Only three months. Still new." Taking a breath, he asked, "What's your poison, Gina?"

She hesitated. "I... I..."

Stephen felt warm, smooth hands slide over his eyes. "Guess who?"

Oh, no. He recognised that voice. His last conquest. *Christ.* "Don't have a damn clue."

"Come on, honey. You can't forget the amazing night we spent together."

His heart raced, blind to the reactions of his two female companions. "I don't know. Truly." He lifted her hands away from his eyes and turned to face the woman. Her eyebrows were well-shaped, and her low cut, white dress was two sizes too small for her. She was gorgeous in a shallow way that didn't come close to Gina.

"It's Anne. How can you not recognise my voice, darling?"

Only because he didn't know her name, but her voice grated in his ears in that high-pitched tone. "Hello. Are you having fun?"

"Of course, darling. When are we catching up? I've been asking about you, but you haven't answered. I understand you're busy."

"I am, and sorry, but I can't." He waved his hand in Gina's direction. "I'd like you to meet Gina and Dalia, two friends of mine."

Anne scowled as she inched her way forward and stroked his cheek. "How about we get out of here and have some real fun?"

Gina laughed, then stormed off, with Dalia following. He couldn't let her get away. "Excuse me." He scurried towards her and tapped her on the shoulder. "Please wait. I still owe you that drink."

She exhaled and touched the base of her throat as if she was nervous. Scanning him from head to toe, she said, "I know your type. Thinks he can sow his wild oats with every woman who might pay him even the tiniest bit of attention. A player. The more notches on his belt, the more he's proud of himself and boasts to his friends. I don't need you to flirt with me because I know who you truly are. Shallow and a plain womaniser. I respect you owning the club, but that doesn't give you the right to bother me about a stupid drink when all you want is to get me in bed. Am I wrong?"

He chuckled. *Wow!* She was a real piece of work, this one. "For your information, you don't know me from a bar of soap, and I am not the shallow person you refer to. If you put aside your judgements, you might learn a thing or two."

"Right. Whatever you say," she said.

Dalia intervened. "Listen, Stephen. We'll come some other night when you've both cooled down. There are obvious misunderstandings here and I apologise for my friend, but she's had a rough time of things."

Gina touched her friend on the shoulder. "Please, Dalia. Let's just leave."

He didn't know what had triggered him and hated himself for being rude to her when she had the right to her opinion. "I am sorry, Gina. I didn't mean to upset you, but I'm not that guy. Really. Let me make it up to you. I'll leave you alone if you promise to enjoy the night without me. I'll stay away."

"I think you should go back to your friend, Anne." She squared her shoulders. "Goodbye."

He watched her leave with her friend, who gave him a reassuring look, then he ambled back to the bar to grab a drink. Anne had left.

He approached the bartender. "When you get a chance, Bruno, give me a vodka, please."

"Sure thing, boss." He grinned as he poured the drink into a glass, gliding it across the counter. "That woman was...interesting. I could hear you guys from over here. She was gorgeous."

He drank the vodka, which soothed his parched throat. "Hmm. If you like the judgemental, negative type, sure."

"I think she likes you."

"Right. Like a swimmer loves a shark. I could see that."

"I know body language, and it was clear she was attracted to you. Don't let her get away. If she made assumptions about you, don't go making assumptions about her."

He chuckled. "You should be my counsellor, Bruno. I don't think I pay you enough. Enjoy the rest of the night."

As he made his way back to his office, Stephen's body slouched. He hated the way the woman had made him feel, despite being drawn to her. At least he knew he wouldn't have to deal with her again. Beauty or not, he didn't need the stress or negativity.

CHAPTER 5

G ina rubbed her eyes, then stretched out her arms as she roused from sleep. A hint of sunlight streamed in through a gap in her curtains. She yawned, her head feeling heavy and body weighing her down. She had struggled to sleep the past two nights and knew exactly why. That creature she'd met on Saturday night had put a sour taste in her mouth. The man was immature and had to throw his flirtatious behaviour right in her face. First, he tried his charms on her, then had the nerve to put on the charm with that other woman. No doubt he was the type who would attempt to get any woman into bed. She would call herself attractive, but she wasn't easy with men and hadn't had sex with anyone in a very long time.

It had been three years since she'd been in a relationship and thinking about that made her sick to her stomach. Her ex-boyfriend before that was aggressive, and luckily, she had the support of friends to keep her safe. No, she had been hurt one too many times, and she refused to let thoughts of a silly player consume her mind.

After rubbing the ache at the back of her neck, she headed to the bathroom, showered, then ate toast and eggs for breakfast. She chewed her last bite, wiped her mouth with a napkin, then went to the bathroom to brush her teeth. The sound of the doorbell made her rush into her room where she picked up her handbag, satchel, and keys.

Making her way to the front door, her heart overflowed with fondness as she smiled at her friend and colleague, Teresa, who was picking her up for their meeting with their possible client, *Katie's Health Group.*

Teresa leaned in and kissed her on the cheek. "Hi, Gina. Are you ready to go, love?" She tilted her heart-shaped face, her vibrant blue eyes scrutinising. Her bob-style haircut and petite frame made her look younger than her thirty-two years.

"I'm ready." Gina locked the door behind her, carried her belongings to Teresa's car, and got in the passenger's side.

Teresa inched her way closer to Gina and squeezed her cheeks. "Oh, darl. You are looking tired these days. Have you had enough sleep?"

Gina sighed. "Not really, but I will survive as always. Now drive."

Teresa shook her head. "I am going to give you some soothing tea that will help you sleep like a baby, and tonight, you are having a warm bath with lavender oils. No arguing."

"Whatever you say, Mother Hen."

"And don't you forget it." She backed out of the driveway and headed to Hawthorn, leaning back in her seat as she thought about her pitch.

"I wish I had more time to research the company, Teresa. John put me on this at the last minute, so I haven't had a chance to find out who works there, not even the director."

"Leave that information to me. I'll be doing the bulk of the presentation, and you can describe how you work. We need to make them feel supported and get them to trust us so we can outshine other digital marketing companies. I spoke to the general manager, Dale, who said the director will be late this morning."

"Well, no one would be in better hands than yours, Teresa. I don't know anyone who'd do a better marketing job." Her friend laughed.

Arriving at the grey, flat-topped building in Hawthorn, Teresa parked on a side-street. They walked for ten minutes, finally reaching a set of steps that led to glass sliding doors. The burly receptionist directed them to the elevators and conference room.

Gina rubbed her hands as she stood at the head of the table while Teresa set down a full-page document about their company.

People dribbled into the room and greeted them. By the time they were all seated, it was time to start. She assumed the empty chair belonged to the director. She didn't even know his name.

Nine staff members surrounded her as she waited for introductions from each of them, four women and five men with friendly eyes on her as they lay out notebooks and pens. She only remembered three names: Jeanie, a myotherapist who appeared to be in her early twenties. Dianne, an older woman who was a practice manager in the city location, and Rob, a middle-aged man who was a physiotherapist. The other names escaped her as her hands sweated with nerves. *Breathe.* She had her reputation to uphold.

The general manager, Dale, fixed his emerald green eyes on her. His posture was tense and his lips pursed. "Great to meet you, Gina and Teresa. You can start as our director will be a tad late. Not sure how long."

Teresa nodded. "Welcome, everyone." Gina's mind turned elsewhere while her friend gave her usual spiel about how they worked from a digital marketing perspective. She stood up straight and waited for her turn, her heart beating a mile a minute. Why was she so nervous? She usually had self-confidence, but this company felt different somehow.

Gina took deep breaths, hating that the tardy director would interrupt the middle of their presentation. In a few minutes, she'd be taking over from her friend. She took calming breaths. The man had no etiquette.

When it was finally her turn, she cleared her throat. "I'm the data scientist on site and I work to incorporate more of the data analysis to inform adjustments of future budgets. I do web and social media analytics and define metrics based on KPIs. In a nutshell, I focus on enhancing marketing effectiveness. This might involve A/B testing, assisting management to work with and understand organisational data, and providing tactical and strategic insights to improve business." Her nerves tensed as it occurred to her that the director was still a no-show. Where was he?

Dianne threaded a hand through her long, blonde hair and looked over at Gina with friendly eyes. "You sound experienced. It sounds like we'll be in expert hands."

"Thank you, Dianne," she said.

Her eyes scanned the room, taking in the staff members until she spotted a familiar figure in the entryway. *Holy hell! It couldn't be.*

The man's eyes roamed the room until they locked onto hers. He raised an eyebrow and sat down with a wave. "Sorry, I'm late, but I had an urgent matter to attend to."

Gina pursed her lips and gripped a pen. *Breathe. Breathe.* His smirk gave her a tight throat and a strong urge to punch the man. He could have come on time, but no, he had to make his damn grand entrance.

"I'm Stephen Farrugiya, the CEO. Don't mind me. Please carry on."

Gina became tongue-tied, legs frozen on the spot as Teresa gently nudged her. Her cheeks were on fire. *I can do this.* Gripping the glass of water on the desk, she sipped quickly and refused to be distracted by the owner of the nightclub. Who would've known he owned a health group too? Was this man made of money?

She ground her teeth and her muscles quivered. "As I said earlier, I'm the data scientist on site and use data analysis to inform adjustments of future budgets." As she repeated herself, heat flushed throughout her body and she plastered a false smile on her face and aimed it in his direction. She drew in slow, steady breaths as she placed a hand over her chest to soften the ache there. A building headache caused her words to jar slightly.

Jeanie cut in, waving red, manicured nails in the air as she finger-brushed her short brown waves. "You seem young, Gina. How much experience could you have had?" She arched a brow and scrutinised her.

Gina's heart raced, but she took a calming breath. "I assure you, I am not that young. I have at least six years of data science experience." She avoided Stephen's eyes, her muscles and jaw already sore from the tension.

Rob nodded with a calm smile, his green eyes friendly. "Your work sounds interesting, Gina." He gave Jeanie a hard look. "We hope to work with you."

She beamed, liking this man instantly. "Thank you, Rob. I take pride in being thorough and put all my focus on the one client in the initial stages."

Stephen waved a hand. "What exactly are your digital marketing strategies, Ms...?"

She shifted her posture, hands sweaty. "It's Cassani, and as for strategies, my coworker, Teresa, already went through that earlier today. Before *you* arrived." The nerve of that man to show up twenty minutes late and interrupt her presentation. She didn't care that he was the CEO. How dare he muddle her thought process? Now she was tongue-tied and couldn't think straight. It was probably because the air conditioner was on low that distracted her from organising her thoughts. Not because of the way this man's muscles pushed through his transparent, white, linen shirt, or the way his sea-blue eyes scanned her from head to toe as if he was trying to figure her out. Definitely not because of those ruby lips.

But why did her mind conjure images of her running her fingers through his subtle beard and moustache, gliding her hands over his flicked-up fringe? No, she hated this guy with a passion. His arrogance dripped all over the table.

Jolting her out of her reverie, Teresa cut in. "I will briefly explain our strategies, Mr Farrugiya. Not a problem at all."

Gina stepped aside and pressed her thumb deeply into her palm. Why had she spoken that way to the man? She was normally polite on a job, but this man pushed all her buttons. A part of her wished they could back out. If she never saw this man again, it would be too soon.

CHAPTER 6

Stephen clasped his hands together as he sat opposite Dale, who watched him in silence three days later. He sorted files on his office desk then made notes about the meeting with Gina and Teresa.

No doubt he was thinking about how rude the woman had been at their formal meeting. He had two minds not to hire them for their services. But then again, other marketers they'd liaised with were not even a fraction better than this company. He'd done his research and liked their reputation and quick results.

A part of him lit up at how he'd broken her icy veneer when he asked for the information, but he could have tried harder to make it on time. Only it wasn't him per se, but then again, he wasn't the type who stuck by the rules. She must have been embarrassed. Her blushes had shown it.

Dale cleared his throat. "What did you think, boss?"

Stephen knit his brows. "They obviously know what they're doing and seem to far outweigh their competitors. I would like to work with them, but..."

His friend chuckled. "The data scientist?"

His heart skipped a beat. "What about her?"

"The tension was steaming between you two. Do you think she'd be able to help?

He shrugged. "She obviously knows her stuff by the way she drilled off those statistics about conversion rates. Oh, and she didn't hesitate when she needed to answer questions. It was as if she knew our businesses better than we do. Not to mention the professional way she structured her presentation, and...what I mean is, if you like the ice queen type, then sure."

Dale held up a hand and tilted his head. "I've never seen you so rattled by someone at work before."

Stephen shook his head, his face heating up. "That's ridiculous. She could've been a tad nicer when I walked in late. Not understanding how busy I am with my other businesses. Sure, she was pretty, but that sharp tongue of hers..."

His friend angled his head. "Wait—are you attracted to her?"

Stephen hesitated. "Like I said, a cold-water fish has more warmth than her, so no."

"You don't sound convincing." Dale's gaze unnerved him. "It was surprising how you got under her skin. You could have been on time, Stephen. Why are you always late?"

He sighed. "A habit, and I don't need anyone to change me. I'm my own person. But then again, this time, it was the investor running late."

"But if we work with them, you'll have to play nice and follow the rules." Dale pointed a finger at him. "She's obviously highly organised and precise, the opposite of you. Wow. That would put a spanner in the works, wouldn't it?"

He loved his friend, but he could be a pain in the arse. "Whatever. What are your thoughts?"

Dale leaned forward. "Their financials are outstanding, and they've won several awards. Even their cost is less than others we've interviewed. I say, let's go for it."

Stephen's posture straightened, adrenaline coursing through his body. But it was only because he was going to enjoy the challenge of breaking down her barriers—and he loved a challenge.

Gina sat in her open-plan office, which featured a long, white desk that ended at large, bare windows with filtered sunlight and a view of the city streets. Teresa sat beside her, and next to her were two creative designers. Opposite them, at another long desk, sat four others who were a mash-up of creatives and technical geeks. Her manager, John, roamed and hovered over his staff.

She loved her desk, which featured a desktop computer, laptop, a potted artificial plant, and a black, ergonomic chair that supported her back well. Suspended lights and more artificial plants hung from the ceiling haphazardly.

Teresa turned to her and flicked through a document. "I've got the quarterly report of that new ecommerce business. It's impressive. Not sure why they need us, but we can improve on their current conversions."

"Great. I'll work on the metrics and send it out later today."

"Okay. And what about the director of *Katie's Health Group*? Did you know he's a billionaire?"

Gina feigned interest. "Is he?" She clicked on her keys and the roar of the printer spurted out a metrics page. "Once I look through these to determine our next steps, I'll email this to them."

"Sure thing," said Teresa. "The health group had been doing well until taking a hit with that staff member committing fraud. Obviously, they need our help. But we can't let that stop us if they hire us." She leaned over to the male colleague beside her and nodded to a question about graphics. Teresa then faced Gina again. "Why haven't we heard anything yet? We gave a great presentation, don't you think?"

"Yes. Apart from his rudeness by showing up late."

"He has a name, you know," said Teresa.

Why were her fingers tingling and her heart racing? She must have been nervous about his judgement of her. She could've behaved more professionally in the meeting, but he knew how to irk her. "Stephen. It must be the name that makes them such jerks."

Teresa laughed. "Just because your ex-boyfriend's name was Steven, docsn't make them all jerks."

Gina put up a hand. "I must say, he's had a lot of success in his health centres and knows how to target his market. But it hasn't always been consistent, and that scandal surely didn't help. He's had an amazing track record for years, so with some slight changes and tweaks, there's potential to do better." She felt sweat at the back of her neck. "But the man is pompous, arrogant, and thinks he rules the world. I admit he is successful, but he could do with a personality make-over." Her cheeks reddened.

Teresa leaned forward. "You fancy the man, don't you? He is handsome."

"Oh, that is ridiculous."

Teresa beamed. "Right. But the way he couldn't take his eyes off you even when I was speaking. There was definite tension between you two. Why are you blushing?"

Gina shook her head. "He would be the last man I'd even consider. I would rather be single for the rest of my life, even if no other man existed."

"Dramatic, isn't it?"

Gina leaned back in her seat, jolted momentarily by the shrill ring of her phone. "Yes, Grace. What's happening?"

"We have a Mr Farrugiya here to meet with you," her receptionist said.

Gina froze and lost her breath. "Right." She fidgeted, then finger-brushed her hair. "Okay. Hold on." Teresa eyed her curiously. "Speaking of the jerk, he's here." She ushered her manager, John, over.

John approached, his grey eyes friendly as he edged closer.

"Are you able to talk to the CEO of *Katie's Health Group*?" Gina asked. "He's asked to see me, but it's better that you talk to him. I'm busy now."

John angled his head. "But if he asked for you, it must be a data science question."

She shook her head. "It's best you go, John. If he has specific questions for me, then I'll talk to him. Let me know." Gina prayed he didn't ask for her, as the less she saw him, the better. She'd been having a good day.

He knit his brows. "We have spoken at least twice, but fine. I will see if he plans to use us. But he will most likely call in your expertise."

She smiled, then spoke back into the phone. "Grace, send him to John's office. He'll be there shortly."

Grace didn't relent. "But he asked for you."

"I know, but it's best he speaks to John for now." A sense of guilt rushed through her because she was obviously ignoring the man. What if this cost them the business? No, doubtful. John would bring him around. He was a charmer.

Teresa patted her on the shoulder. "Why are you avoiding the man? He must have questions for you."

Gina winced. "John's got this."

Teresa rose. "I'm sure he does."

"A part of me wants him not to hire us, but another part knows it's great for business."

Teresa laughed as she typed into her computer and waving off a joke made by one of her colleagues. Gina gazed over her shoulder, wondering why he'd asked to see her rather than the manager.

She didn't know how long she'd been daydreaming when a tap on her shoulder alerted her to John, who stood opposite with dilated eyes.

"What is it?" Gina asked, with the others looking on.

"He's hired us but would still like to speak with you about how you work. You're now in charge of this new project, so scoot on over and continue to wow him." Her shoulders deflated. "Don't give me that look. I can get Teresa to lead this project, but she's leading the other account. Head on over to my office and take your time. I've got a client meeting."

"Yes, sir," Gina replied. She made her way down the corridor in slow steps, wanting to turn back. Butterflies in her stomach made her sick until she reached John's office. Guarded, she opened the door and took calming breaths. His broad shoulders gave him presence and the scent of musk and spices was unnerving.

Stephen turned, his eyes riveted on her. "Thanks for seeing me on such short notice. I assume your boss told you we'd like to hire your firm?" She nodded. "Great. I do like to get on with things."

Gina sat in John's chair and bit her bottom lip. Her feet shuffled under the desk. "Fine." His open-necked red shirt revealed blonde chest hairs and the tight-fitting blue pants clung to him like a second skin, all toned.

"Your manager, John, mentioned that you're the lead on this campaign, so explain to me the first steps before we sign up."

This man oozed arrogance but she would not be taken in by his charm. She ignored her increased heart rate and parched throat. "Surely, John explained all that."

"In a manner, but I'd like your take on things. If you don't mind."

"Okay, Mr Farrugiya. But I expect certain rules of our business to be maintained."

His eyes lit up. "And what would those rules be, Gina?"

"The name is Ms Cassani."

He put up a hand, his eyes darkening. "Of course, Ms...Cassani. The rules?"

She rubbed her hands together, the warmth of her neck making her brain fuzzy. What were those damn rules again? Her mind became blank. *Rules, Gina. Rules.* His scrutinising gaze made her physically sick. Why was he staring that way? Get yourself together. You can do this. "One rule, Mr Farrugiya, is that if we make an appointment, we expect punctuality. Also, if we ask for quarterly reports by a specific date, we expect that to be done."

He nodded, glancing at her lips. "Of course. Now, explain the initial steps and the information you need from us."

She could do facts. "After you sign our contracts and terms of agreement, we will require your monthly financials to establish a baseline. Are you wanting us to focus on a particular business, or provide a general overview?"

"Only those in targeted areas within *Katie's Health Group*. I'll give you a list. As I said to John, we focus on preventative and holistic care, which means that it needs to be clear to our target audience and demographics what our mission is."

"Right. Where do we start?"

"As I mentioned in the meeting, we run several health centres that feature myotherapy, chiropractice, holistic health, physiotherapy services, and podiatry. The holistic, preventative healthcare is crucial to our brand."

Gina was curious about how he averted his gaze at his emphasis on the word, holistic. Something had affected the man, but what? "Okay, then. We will work towards improved user experience and potentially create a health hub campaign to drive new customers to the service. Increase your visibility, mainly in holistic and preventative care. We will focus on your website design to ensure it's optimal." She continued her spiel, then waited with bated breath.

"Sounds amazing. But for me to work with anyone, I like to get to know staff members on a personal level. It helps to develop a rapport, and with that, an improved working relationship and experience."

The nerve of the man. "I expect us to be professional, Mr Farrugiya. We do not do personal in business. Now, if you don't mind, please see Grace, who will draw up contracts for you to sign."

Stephen stood up abruptly. "Not a problem." He sauntered out without a backward glance, and she was curious about how much of a problem he was going to be. His self-inflated ego would make sure he gave her a hard time, but she would maintain her composure and not let the man win.

CHAPTER 7

Stephen's senses sharpened as he sat side by side with Gina in his office, taking in her peppermint and cinnamon scent. He pulled out a thick sheaf of files from his cluttered desk and dropped pens and a notebook. Stacks of health books and other stationery items littered the desk. His office door was transparent glass, so he could see his office staff, who managed the individual health centres.

Clicking into his computer, he turned to Gina, whose eyebrows rose at the sight of the state of his desk. "As the demographics show, qualities vary depending on the service. But I'd like you to first focus on holistic healthcare: Pilates, clinical exercise, dietetics, and physiotherapy." He clicked into another tab, displaying a graph. "This is the number of online and phone enquiries we've had in the last few years, and the conversion rates. Apart from that slight dip because of the scandal I'm sure you heard about."

Gina nodded. "Still impressive. But there is room for improvement, especially with local health hubs that can assess the target group. If you wouldn't mind sending your financials from these areas, too." She pointed over a small map unfolded on his desk. "We can organise a mobile health service in these areas that have had a decrease with enquiries to increase visibility." She pointed to the screen and her arm brushed his. "Why the dip here?"

Her cheeks blazing, his gaze lingered, but she averted her eyes. Her beauty distracted him. "Our website changed, and not for the better, so that definitely needs revamping. Even our social media reach could do with some work."

"I will get Teresa to work on that, and I'll arrange A/B testing after analysing your target profiles. My research of the metrics will also be about advising your team to fully understand your market and train you to understand the organisational data."

He peered at his Rolex. Lunchtime. His stomach rumbled. "How about we take a break and grab lunch? It's one o'clock."

She abruptly rose. "No, I can leave and come back."

He waved a hand. "There is a cafe across the road that makes the best burgers. We can head out for an hour and walk back. Easy peasy."

Gina frowned and peered past him as if processing. "Fine. Let's go. We shouldn't waste much time."

He forced a smile, wondering why she had to be such a hard taskmaster. Did she ever wind down and stop thinking? He was determined to break down her veneer. She likely didn't know the meaning of fun.

As they stepped inside the elevator, there was an awkward silence. Gina stood cross-armed and gazed at the ground. The thick tension made him wonder if he'd done the right thing, as he obviously didn't impress her as a man.

Stephen glanced at her tanned legs beneath a tight-fitted brown skirt, and her white blouse buttoned to the top. The curved outline of her neck and rich, auburn hair triggered a need to glide his hands over them. Even her lopsided grin enhanced her beauty, and he wanted to get lost in those rich, brown eyes, which were the colour of chocolate. What was wrong with him? He shouldn't be thinking about his coworker that way. Most likely because he hadn't had fun with anyone in a month, when his record usually involved having a new woman with no strings attached every fortnight. It was easier to have superficial relationships without the pain of inevitable loss.

The sultry breeze outside brushed his cheeks as they crossed the road. The revving of engines and tooting of horns grounded him.

He swung open the door of the café, and his hunger increased with the smells of fresh coffee, spices, and hot, char-grilled foods.

The regular youthful male server smiled in greeting. "Welcome, Stephen. Take a seat."

"Thanks Mick. Not too busy today?"

He shook his head. "We've passed our rush hour." He handed them menus. "I'll be back in a few."

Stephen sat opposite Gina, whose straightened shoulders would likely prevent her from having back problems. The tables were close together in rows of two, with an upstairs room and a counter behind him. Muffled laughter and conversation rang out from three other tables. He stared at the menu for a few minutes, wondering if she would ever talk. "What interests you?"

She knit her brow as she looked up at him. "I'll have the chicken salad."

Mick walked to their table. "What can I get you guys?"

Stephen watched Gina pick at a nail as if nervous. "A chicken salad for the lady and a burger and fries for me, thanks Mick."

Gina sighed. "I'll have a mineral water too"

"Also a strong cappuccino, Mick. Thanks." The server walked off with a nod before Stephen realised Gina was shaking her head.

"I can order for myself. I am quite capable," she said.

He swallowed. "I'm sorry, but I knew what you were having, so I ordered for you." What was wrong with this woman? Did she ever smile?

The buzzing of her phone inside her bag distracted her, so she pulled it out and scrolled through. *Okay. Rude.* Was she going to spend all of lunch on the phone while he wanted a simple conversation?

After five minutes passed and she was still texting someone, he had to say something. "You mentioned being a data scientist for six years. That's quite a bit of experience."

She glanced up from her phone. "It is." Turning back to it, she finished the text, then put it back inside her bag.

"Is it something you've always wanted to do?"

She nodded. "Yes. I love facts, numbers, metrics, and machine learning. I initially wanted to focus on medical research, but then learned about data science, which is a newer branch of science. I wanted to break into something innovative and creative too. People might think numbers are not creative, but they can be."

"The marketing strategies are creative. Assessing and testing different approaches. It is interesting work." Her dark eyes lit up, and he wanted to see more of that.

Mick set their drinks on the table along with two plates. "Enjoy."

"Thanks, Mick." Stephen picked up his burger and devoured it, the sauce dripping down his chin. Quickly wiping it away after seeing Gina's eyebrow raise, he laughed on the inside. Did he make her nervous? No. She hated him with a passion, and was only with him because of their work together. Not by choice.

Gina forked her chicken salad, chewing slowly and precisely, then dabbed at her mouth to wipe away crumbs.

There was that awkward silence again. "I appreciate you helping us. We have had difficulties getting the numbers we wanted for the health group. But my other businesses are doing well."

She lifted a brow. "What are your other businesses?"

Stephen's heart soared at her interest in his work. At last, she had softened her tone. "I have ecommerce businesses in coffee, clothing, and jewellery. But if they decrease in profits, I'll know who to call."

"I have had experience marketing coffee brands and jewellery, but not clothing. I do like to try data science in a range of industries. You learn so much about the fields, and it inspires more of my creativity."

"You do light up when talking about your work. What else makes you happy?"

She cleared her throat. "I think we should hurry with our food and not linger too long. There's a lot to do, and I don't want to be wasting time."

He didn't think sharing their lives was a waste of time, but each to their own. Her thick veneer was back, and he had to be patient. But then, why did he even care when they were total opposites? She would drive him crazy with her incessant judgements about his life, and he couldn't live that way. No, she might be amazing to look at, but it would stop there. They would maintain their working relationship and nothing else.

CHAPTER 8

On Saturday morning Gina munched on a Caesar salad outside a local restaurant accompanied by Teresa and Dalia. She thought about the last few days working with Stephen, not able to get his searing blue eyes or strong-looking, muscular hands out of her head. Not to mention the way he swaggered with zest and confidence, bordering on arrogance, yet with a hint of sexiness. What was wrong with her? She had to get him out of her head. He was much too childish and carefree for her liking.

"Earth to Gina," said Teresa.

She beamed in her direction. "Sorry, what?"

"I asked, when are you seeing Stephen again? For the next step in the campaign?"

Her cheeks warmed and tingled. "In a few days I'll get the health hub set up, then work on the proposed metrics. Why do you ask?"

"I don't know. Ever since starting this campaign, you've been distracted. What's going on with you?"

Dalia intervened. "Ooh, I know exactly what it is." She grinned, then turned to Teresa as if they had a secret code. "She's infatuated."

Gina winced. "What are you talking about?"

"The CEO, Stephen. He is attractive and seems to have taken a shine to you, love. It wouldn't hurt to nurture yourself a bit and focus on self-care. We all need a balance of work, rest, and love," said Teresa.

"Right. So my self-care would be to indulge in an unequal relationship whereby the male is irresponsible, childish, arrogant, and a womaniser. Is that what you call balance, Teresa?"

"Well, when you put it that way...yes," she said.

Dalia flicked her fringe away from her eye, then put her fork down beside her rigatoni dish. "No harm in becoming good friends and seeing where it leads. He seemed like a nice guy at the nightclub. I'd say he's accomplished a lot and is successful. Noble qualities."

"Like I said, he's a billionaire, Gina," said Teresa. "There could be worse things in life, but first and foremost you cannot burn yourself out with only work. You need to enjoy yourself, too."

Teresa had a point. Gina had lost all semblance of joy three years ago when her ex-boyfriend betrayed her in the worst possible way. Despite having excelled in her career by twenty-eight years of age, a deep empty pit in her stomach was a recurring feeling. No, she would never trust a man again. "I have all my friends and my work, and that's enough for me."

Teresa rubbed her hands together. "How is your artwork going?"

Her shoulders squared. "Great. I have a few pieces done and am working on a personal piece that's helping me to express feelings I've been struggling with."

"You need to get your work into a gallery," said Dalia.

Gina rested back in her seat and stared into her glass. "I don't have enough pieces, Dalia. Of course, it would be a dream come true, but are they even good enough?"

Dalia threaded a hand through her copper-coloured hair. "That doesn't matter. At least get the interest of a curator for your work. Get the ball rolling, my dear." Dalia's warm chestnut eyes matched her personality, caring and open. Her triangular-shaped face and high cheekbones gave her model-like qualities.

Gina had to do this right and refused to ask for interest until she was emotionally ready and had enough pieces to submit. It was too soon. "I have enough to do with this new campaign, Dalia, so it's not my priority right now."

Teresa leaned forward. "How about we visit a gallery for inspiration? It might help you complete more paintings to submit to galleries a lot quicker?"

She stared at the ground, a pang of anxiety flickering in her stomach. "I do not need inspiration," Gina lied.

"That's fine then. We can still go. How about it? There's a small art gallery close to where your sister worked years ago. It's also coincidentally near Stephen's workplace."

Her heart rate increased, and her hands sweated. Swallowing, she shook her head. "I am not going anywhere that reminds me of her. I don't want to talk about Toni either. It's not up for discussion." The looks on her friends' faces instilled a sense of guilt as she hadn't meant to raise her voice or take out her frustrations on to them. "I'm sorry, but can we change the subject please?"

She was happy to live her life without being reminded of her sister ever again. Despite Toni's incessant calls and apologies, Gina would never forgive her.

Stephen and Dale stepped inside the spacious clinical exercise room. Dumbbells, treadmills, rowing machines, massage balls, and rollers arranged around them. Thin mats lined the wall while three male patrons twisted and turned their upper limbs under the instruction of one of the physiotherapists. The smell of sweat combined with cologne permeated the air. Glass doors displayed a busy street outside.

"Stretch out those arms and breathe. Do three more on either side, then work on the lower limb exercises I showed you. I'll be a minute," Joel said, turning to Stephen and Dale. "Hey, guys. What brings you two by?"

Stephen glanced at one huffing man who had water dripping from his face and arms. Another two jumped effortlessly on the mat without breaking a sweat, obviously fitter.

He had become more interested in preventative and holistic health after his former fiancée, Katie, had died of a heart attack. It had happened five years ago, but he still remembered that most traumatic day of his life. He ignored the clenching in his gut. "Remember, I mentioned we'd be running a campaign to increase business?"

"Sure. You wanted to target this area after a downturn in enquiries. Is something happening?" Joel stood cross-armed, watching the men behind him.

"Yes. You'll be getting a call from Gina, who's from a marketing firm. She'll ask you about the latest enquiries and conversions. But we also wanted to give you a heads-up about your involvement in possibly having a mobile health hub in some of the rural areas. It'll run for a few weeks. I'd like to help the indigenous community access healthcare, and this is one way to start. I'd potentially like to open a permanent clinic in one of the rural areas."

Joel nodded. "Sounds great. I am definitely down to helping those in need."

Dale patted him on the shoulder. "You might decide to stay in the bush."

Joel shook his head. "I doubt it. My place is in the city, but I am happy to take part. Give me the details. We'll need a replacement here while I'm gone."

"Of course. I've got someone in mind," said Stephen. "I will let you get back to your clients. Thanks, Joel." They waved to each other, then headed out to Stephen's sporty ash-black car.

Dale climbed into the passenger seat and Stephen started the motor then drove along the congested main road. "That mobile van. Whose idea was that?"

Stephen gripped the steering wheel as he glanced over at his friend, knowing he would never have come up with such a great idea. "It was Gina's idea. She thinks that us getting more involved in the regional communities can give us more visibility and facilitate not only the indigenous community, but also new markets around the city. We need to fill those gaps." Her beautiful, rich, dark eyes flashed in his mind and a lightness in his chest revived his energy. Why couldn't he get that annoying woman out of his mind?

Dale laughed. "Wow. You do like her, don't you?"

Stephen scoffed. "Don't be ridiculous." He cut in front of a slow truck driver, who beeped his horn. Bumper to bumper traffic made him sigh. "I am so inclined to improve infrastructure here. It's a nightmare in Richmond."

"Hmm, but don't change the subject. I can tell you're attracted to her. She might tame your wild ways."

Stephen turned to him. "My ways are not wild. I am just me, enjoying life and not having to worry about a woman who is obviously trouble. I have never met anyone so negative about life. It's exhausting."

"And it's exhausting having to watch you sleep with a multitude of women just to forget. It's unhealthy."

"Noted." He sped up on reaching the freeway and breathed a sigh of relief. "Listen. I was thinking about going to that national gallery near our work. Apparently, they're having an exhibition in the next few weeks. Care to join?"

"I'll let you know. Are you still looking for artwork for your living room?"

"I am, but I want an abstract piece that makes me feel something. Strong emotions."

"You mean the feelings that you happily avoid the rest of the time?"

Stephen punched him in the shoulder. "Shut it, Dale. I'm still your boss and can fire your stupid butt."

"Oh, no, you love me too much. Who else would put up with you?"

Stephen chuckled as he kept his eyes on the freeway and headed to another clinic that had suffered a downturn in visitors after Katie died. If only he'd seen the signs. Pushing aside the ache in his chest, he thought about seeing Gina again at work on Monday. He wondered how she was spending her Saturday. Not that he cared.

CHAPTER 9

Gina watched her boss, John, a tall, imposing man, with his hands by his sides as he jutted out his chin and spoke to Stephen. She sat with her hands in her lap in the conference room at Stephen's place of business. Three female colleagues and two males were also present, engrossed in the interchange between the two men. Teresa sat beside her.

John turned to her. "Break down the financials for us, Gina."

Her foot rested firmly on glossy lino hybrid flooring as her eyes darted around the room. "Checking *Katie's Health Group* financials, I found that over the last three years, you've had a decline in enquiries, and those enquiries resulted in a twenty-five per cent conversion rate, so not great. When I went back five years business was booming, until it wasn't. Something caused the shift." She was curious and stopped in her tracks as Stephen's complexion turned pale. He rubbed hard around the back of his neck and undid a button on his shirt as if he couldn't get enough air. What was going on with him?

Regaining his composure, Stephen said, "Which area is the one we need to target first?" He appeared to be an expert at shutting off his emotions.

Gina's heart melted for no apparent reason. She must be tired to be wanting to soothe him. This guy was trouble. "I say we work on Geelong to start."

Teresa intervened. "Which means I'll be focusing on marketing strategies to target the different social needs and demographics. Gina can start the mobile health hubs in Geelong, and I'll focus on the other urban areas you listed."

"Sounds good," said Stephen.

John angled his head towards Stephen. "I understand you're planning to oversee a health centre in New Zealand—is that right?"

Stephen nodded. "Yes, sir. It's an established business but we'll need to finalise the details with the owner. I would appreciate input to prepare for the opening."

Her boss gazed at Gina. "You've always wanted to travel to New Zealand, so here's your chance."

Gina's heart beat fast. "Excuse me, John?"

"Now's the perfect time to plan a prelaunch of the business and build buzz before opening day. You'll create new projections but it'll take you out of the country."

She swallowed. "But what the about the health hub in Geelong? That will keep me busy." Gina knew about his initiative in New Zealand, but she never expected it would happen this soon. Why hadn't he told her it was their focus too? He was a man of mystery.

"Stephen and I discussed this, and we've agreed to start the Geelong hub before New Zealand. Teresa can monitor Geelong, or we'll get Julie or Mary. We're a team on this. It'll only be a temporary thing. A week at most." His eyes roamed the room. "Let's build up the excitement before the grand opening. When are you planning to open the new centre?"

Stephen nodded. "In about a month."

"How does that sound?" asked John.

Gina's shoulders sank. "Well..." Why did she not look forward to spending time with the man? "But wouldn't Teresa be the better fit for New Zealand?"

Teresa shook her head. "I have family commitments, Gina. I can't make it work."

John put up a hand. "It's settled then." He turned to Gina. "But if you still have reservations, we can discuss it privately."

Stephen glanced in her direction and smirked as if he'd won a sick game. Why did he push her buttons? He was like a dog who'd got all his bones. *Game on.*

Gina swallowed her pride. She would be professional, as she always was. She wouldn't let Stephen put her guard up. "It's fine, John. All good," she lied.

At the end of the meeting, she scurried out, hating the way Stephen made her feel. Not like herself. Mushy and soft. She needed to go for a walk and clear her head without having him on her mind day and night. What was wrong with her? He was a womaniser, and no doubt he'd see her as a challenge. But it wasn't as if she'd give in to his charms. Not a chance in hell. She was smarter and too responsible for that.

Stepping into the elevator during her lunch break, she walked through the sliding doors and made her way across the road and busy streets towards the Alexandra Gardens. She found a bench and rested back against its hard surface.

Palm trees leaned on either side as she sat opposite the Yarra River and drew calmness into her chest to shut out her thoughts. Nature had always evoked a stillness in her and helped her recharge. It was her way of forgetting her problems, particularly when Stephen triggered her and made her think of the past.

If only she didn't need to work with him...but what choice did she have? She had always been an achiever and followed the rules, doing the right things, so why steer away from that when it wasn't in her nature?

Sunlight cast sectioned shadows across the rippling water, and noises behind her made her turn towards cyclists and pedestrians taking leisurely strolls. The view of the towering buildings congested as a backdrop to the huddle of trees and boats along the banks of the river. The gentle wind brought balance.

The snap of a twig and footsteps made her peer over her shoulder. She winced. "What are you doing here?"

Stephen stood awkwardly with his hands in his pockets. "Teresa mentioned you like coming to this park, so I thought we could clear the air." He shifted his feet then slowly made his way to the bench, as if seeking her permission. "May I sit here?"

She shrugged. "It's a free country."

He sat close to the edge of the bench to give her space, but despite that, she couldn't help getting short of breath and on edge as she clasped her hands tightly in her lap. His own breath seemed to have quickened. "Why do you hate me so much?"

She flinched, not expecting his words. "I don't hate you. I don't even know you, but you and I need to tolerate each other during this campaign."

"Tolerate sounds negative to me. You have something against me, so I'd like for us to resolve things before we get further into our work." He sighed and stared out over the water. "You don't know me, so I don't want you to make assumptions about me, Gina."

She scoffed. "What I can see is someone who is arrogant, too sure of himself, and stuck in the Peter Pan phase of his life."

He laughed. "Wow. So much for you not knowing me when you make such judgements. If that's how you feel, let's focus on what's best for my company, given we are paying you substantially. But for the record, I have worked damn hard to get to where I am and want you to know..."

She turned to him and saw a darkness in his eyes. "Want me to know what?"

He fidgeted with his hands and took a deep breath. "Nothing. It's all good. Let's change the subject."

She shifted. "You didn't need to follow me to the park. We could've discussed this at the office." A part of her lied, not wanting him to leave after she'd seen him falter with his words. Was there more to the man than met the eye? The vulnerability in his gaze made her heart lurch.

"I will leave if you want me to leave, but first, I'd like to resolve things between us. We need to work amicably and be professional about this. I don't want you to profess you know me when you don't." She remained silent. "Let's work peacefully."

"Fine," she said.

He knit his brows. "It is beautiful here. It reminds me of New Zealand with all its greenery and hilly landscapes."

Had she judged him too harshly? Could she give him the benefit of the doubt? They didn't need to be friends, but they could work well together professionally. "What's so special about New Zealand?"

He hesitated. "The peace and culture." He bowed his head and briefly closed his eyes. "I have to go. I'll see you back at the office."

Gina nodded. "Okay." She watched the way he rushed off without looking back at her, as if she'd said something wrong. What was it about New Zealand that made him wistful, and why did he feel the need to leave so abruptly? A man with his own demons?

CHAPTER 10

Stephen's sneakers dug into the moist, finely cut grass at their temporary market stall in Geelong, with its marquee-covered roof, and stand showcasing brochures, flyers, business cards, merchandise, and health products from *Katie's Health Group*. A row of four plastic white chairs were lined up nearby to allow passersby to have a free massage from Jeanie the myotherapist, and Joel, his physiotherapist. Dale stood on the other side, schmoozing with a young woman who couldn't stop staring at him.

The blue sky and scorching sunshine warmed Stephen's scalp as Gina reached for dollar notes while she handed a customer a small stress ball, a heat bead, and a business card. Others lined up while she gave her best smile, pointing to Jeanie, who leaned forward to explain her form of massage for particular ailments.

Gina gave her spiel. "This is Stephen, the owner of the health centres. He owns and is in charge of ten centres around Victoria, and plans to open up new centres in the regional areas, as well as New Zealand, which will be the first international location."

"Impressive," said a stocky woman, who was listening nearby.

"What we are offering here," added Gina, "is a trial. If you will sit over there, we can offer you a free massage in exchange for half price on any of our health services, excluding yoga. We have a centre here in Geelong that's close by. Take our business card." She handed her the card.

"Thank you. I wouldn't mind a free massage," said the woman, and made her way to the chair where Jeanie lay her hands on her shoulders.

They had a view of the sea and Cunningham Pier, with a ferry boat about to leave the port. Groups of people entered the boat while others lay picnics on the grass, or entered the many fine restaurants and cafes surrounding the space. A line of people stood in an area that offered helicopter rides.

Stephen couldn't help but admire Gina's tight black t-shirt, which pressed nicely against her slim body above loose white shorts that fell to her smooth, tanned knees. She smelled of honey and cinnamon, and he yearned to thread his hands through the wispy strands of hair on the long outline of her neck. *Stop. Why am I having erotic thoughts about this woman who hates me?*

His stomach rumbled. When no further customers approached, he took the chance to have a break after standing in the sun for two hours. He locked eyes with Gina, standing awkwardly by his side and straightening up the flyers along the stand. "You did well, Gina. Thanks for arranging all this. It's great marketing for us."

She cleared her throat. "It's my job," she said stiffly.

"I know, but still. I know how much work you've put into this. It's amazing. We've drawn such a crowd. Thank you." A redness crept up her neck, but she remained silent.

"Hey, Gina," interrupted Dale. "I love what Teresa did to our website with those fancy pop-ups. It should help draw in new subscribers."

"Thanks, Dale. Teresa is brilliant with that stuff. She's quite creative." She intermittently peered at Stephen.

He wanted to spend time alone with her. They were in a captivating part of Victoria, and could get to know each other better. She wasn't all negative when she spoke about things she loved, which was obviously her marketing work.

He dove in. "How about we grab lunch? There's a nice seafood restaurant a few minutes away, which I recommend. I'm sure we can come back in an hour and resume our duties." Stephen turned to Jeanie and Joel. "You guys don't mind?"

Joel said, "No, go on ahead."

Jeanie dug into the shoulders of another patron having a massage. But, sporadically she would glare at Gina. Was she jealous when there was nothing to be jealous about?

Gina waved. "No, you go. I'd rather stay here. I am not hungry." She shifted further away from him and kicked at the blades of grass. She then reached for her bag, retrieved her mobile phone and scrolled through the display. Was she avoiding him?

Dale approached her. "You should go have lunch with Stephen and make sure he eats. You don't want to be around him when he's hungry. He's like a car without petrol, running on empty. There's plenty of us here. We'll go next."

Gina put her phone back inside her bag. "I don't know, Dale."

He waved. "Come on. Go. You deserve a break."

She hesitated, but then nodded. "Okay then."

Stephen climbed the five timber steps that led to the open door of the seafood restaurant as they made their way inside to be greeted by a towering waitress. She smiled and walked to a square table in a booth with a leather backrest on the seat, and small windows surrounding the space letting in a hint of sunshine. Paintings of the sea and the Geelong landscape lined the walls above the tables. Glossy lino flooring gave the restaurant a spacious feel.

Peering through the menus, Stephen knew what he planned to order. "I've had their seafood chowder, and it is to die for."

Gina gave him a neutral look. "Fine. I'll have the same."

The waitress approached and took their order, her eyes lingering on Stephen before she walked away. If he wasn't so entranced by the woman opposite him, he'd have taken her number.

Gina cleared her throat and watched the waitress with curiosity. Was she jealous? "It will be interesting to see how today goes with your Geelong centre. See whether we can convert more enquiries into sales."

Stephen nodded. "It's been an amazing turn-out," he said. "You've outdone yourself."

She sighed. "As I said earlier, I am only doing my job. I don't need your flattery."

His chest tightened. *Here we go again*. What was her problem? Couldn't she relax and accept a compliment? "I know you don't, but I have never used a marketing company before. It's only after..."

She angled her head, as if curious.

He steeled himself. Talking about Katie always brought pain, and he would much rather put it behind him. But she deserved to know the truth about his late fiancée. Only because it would help ensure they kept honouring her in business. No other reason. "My fiancée, Katie." He squared his shoulders. "She died five years ago." Stephen averted his eyes. "After she died, things went sour. My staff was affected. It impacted business at the time, which was why we took that sudden dip. They loved her."

Gina's eyes had softened when he looked back at her. "I am so sorry, Stephen. I wondered where the name came from."

He clenched his hands. The gut-wrenching pain in his chest felt like a vice. "Anyway, enough about that. How are you enjoying your day?"

Gina bit her bottom lip and her eyes darkened. "I don't mind challenges and problems to be solved, so...I'm having fun."

"You have fun solving problems?"

She shrugged. "Why not? As a billionaire yourself, you've fought many challenges. How big are you planning to make *Katie's Health Group*?"

His heart warmed, relieved she had relaxed a little in his company. "I'd like to work towards targeting disadvantaged places overseas too, but first, I'll work through the regional parts of Victoria and New Zealand."

The waitress intervened with their glasses of Shiraz. "Here you go. I'll be back shortly with your food." Stephen smiled, but quickly avoided her eyes that lingered.

"Teresa's focusing on the list of areas most in need of your services, so once they're taken care of, you can move on from those locations. Start there. She plans to arrange mobile health vans that give easy access, especially to those who are elderly or disabled. Even those who don't drive. We need to target all possibilities and barriers."

"Great. Teresa works a goldmine too."

"Yes, she's amazing, and we work well together." She sipped a little wine. "You must work well with Dale. How long have you two been friends?"

"Oh, gosh. A long time. Since we were in primary school. We got into a lot of mischief growing up."

"I can imagine," said Gina. "What kind of mischief did you get into?"

Stephen had to cast his mind back. "I once put a frog inside my teacher's bag. You should have seen her face when she put her hand inside. She screamed and ran out of the classroom. When she returned with the principal, they immediately knew it was me because I was always the one pranking the classroom. But I loved being the jokester. Life's too serious and boring otherwise."

She shook her head. "You might as well call me boring because I would never have done such a childish thing."

"No, I imagine you were the type who might have been the teacher's pet. Always finishing her work on time, making sure to study hard for tests. I bet that even if you got ninety per cent on your exam, you'd still be mad at yourself."

Gina swallowed and peered past him. "You don't know me."

"I know enough to imagine you would be like that."

The waitress returned with their steaming seafood chowder, which was served in bowls made of Vienna bread. Inside were prawns, scallops, mussels, calamari, fish, and octopus, swimming in a creamy garlic and spring onion sauce.

Stephen devoured his, the smooth texture of prawns with a hint of herbs and cream dancing on his palate. The hot soup was full of flavour. "How is it?"

Gina put down her spoon. "Tasty, with just enough salt. It's good." She swallowed the liquid and wiped a remnant of scallop from her chin. He yearned to kiss her and was jealous of the spoon, curious about how her lips would taste against his own. He wondered how her whole body would feel against his. But he had to put aside his emotions and remain professional. She would only hurt him in the end.

CHAPTER 11

Though she was still curious about his late fiancée, Katie, he had gone and ruined things. Gina couldn't believe he would assume that he knew her like that. He had implied she was boring. But in her eyes, she was a stickler for rules, and doing the right thing, and would never resort to childish behaviour like Stephen had back in high school. Even now, he had to take a light-hearted approach to everything, but if she behaved that way, it could cost her her job, and without it, she'd be a failure. She already considered herself to be a partial failure, given her lack of courage to showcase her art. But she couldn't get past the fear that galleries would reject her. How would she cope with her life's work being discarded like that? She was afraid she'd stop painting if her work was not good enough.

As for her companion opposite, the way he brushed a strand away from his eye or the muscular outline of his large hands gave her a sharp tingle in her chest. The way his blue eyes lit up at the pleasure of savouring his soup and how his robust muscles rippled beneath his cream t-shirt made her sick with desire. What was going on with her?

It was ludicrous to even think about this man romantically when they were opposites and barely tolerated each other. She had to be nice to him for the sake of her work, so that's all this would be. A pleasant lunch between client and employee, a project which would be over in a few months. He'd be a distant memory once their work was done. All that mattered was success in her career.

She relished the rest of her soup and noticed Stephen staring as she brought her glass of cold wine to her lips. "What is it?"

He looked away. "Nothing. I'd like a coffee before we go. How about you?"

She nodded. "All right."

He flagged down the waitress, who arrived quickly. "I'd like a strong cappuccino."

"A hot chocolate," added Gina.

The waitress beamed in his direction. "Of course. Any dessert?" They shook their heads.

Gina scrutinised him as he leaned forward and wiped the corners of his lips with a napkin. She liked the thick shape of his lips. *Stop.*

Stephen pulled at the round neck of his t-shirt. "It is hot in here, don't you think?"

"I don't think so," she lied. The heat in her body was intense despite the air-conditioning, but it must have been on low. The silence between them was unnerving. "I love the landscape here in Geelong. It's a sight to see. The only issue is the parking problem and the swarms of people who can't keep their distance. Not to mention the graffiti and pollution. A lot needs to be done by the local council."

Stephen nodded. "It's not only Geelong, but the entire world, Gina. How about you focus on the good things for today? Not everything has to be negative."

She scoffed. "I am a realist, Stephen. Without my multi-focus, nothing would get fixed. I have written several letters to the MPs about the lack of parking and the vandalism, but all I got was 'we have a plan in place', and nothing more. I have seen little improvement over the last few years. Have you?"

He shrugged. "I haven't noticed. As you can see, I've been busy running my businesses and setting up a new one overseas. If you had to fix the global issues of the world, you wouldn't be living your life. Live your life, Gina."

Her chest ached. "I live my life, and responsibly at that."

"Okay then." The waitress set down their hot beverages before walking off. "Tell me, Gina. What do you do outside of work? Any hobbies or interests?"

She might as well make conversation despite not appreciating his tone. *Remember: he is the client.* "I enjoy jogging a few times a week, crossword puzzles, and art."

He angled his head. "Really? I love two of those things: jogging and art. Right now, I'm looking for a landscape painting for my home and a few for the nightclub. Can you recommend any artists?"

Gina's shoulders relaxed at learning he loved art too. "Tom Roberts or Frederick McCubbin, if you like Australia's history with challenges of the bush or farm life. McCubbin painted the sadder side of people's relationships with the landscape. *The Pioneer* is famous because of its expression of humanity fighting against the bush and rural life. But there's also William Robinson, who loved to paint strong, detailed images of the Australian bushland. One in particular, *Numimbah with Blue Pools,* gives you a sense of the vastness of the land with a broad, big picture perspective. The subtle shades are brilliant and hard to capture. If only I could..."

Stephen tucked his hand under his chin and glanced at her lips. "If only you could what?"

"Nothing." She wasn't about to tell him she was a painter when he would most likely judge her work as not good enough. No, she wouldn't take the risk. They had to maintain their professional relationship.

"How about I get you to choose a painting for me? Consider it part of your job."

She clasped her hands together. "I don't think so. I have enough to do with the marketing campaign. No time." Heat suffused her cheeks. This was getting too personal for her liking. Gina sipped her steaming drink.

He drank down most of his. "We'll make time. I don't expect you to work weekends, and I'd be happy to attend a gallery with you. Isn't there one here?"

She shook her head. "No time today, but I'm sure you'll find the perfect painting. You don't need me when you love art yourself, and most likely know what you'd be buying."

"I love Michael Fitzjames."

She nodded. "He is amazing too. The way he shows how the world is like a veil. How the reality of life is about death."

"Agreed, but it's as if the more you stare at his paintings, the more you see. The detail is out of this world."

"Exactly. The way the sky changes the longer you look at it. It gives me that sense of bliss and living in the moment."

He chuckled. "They're meaningful and surreal." He placed a finger on his chin. "I have noticed that you become a different person when talking about art. How did you get interested in it?"

Her heart fluttered. "Since I was a child. I remember when my dad took me to my first art gallery. He loved art. I was only twelve. I fell in love with the depth of perception, the different strokes of the brush, the contrast of light and dark. But when I leave that world, I find a world that doesn't capture the same beauty. Art draws me into a different space, full of colour and possibilities. Full of wonder."

His eyes lit up. "There is beauty in everything if you look hard enough." He looked at the window. "For instance, that sunlight through the glass forms a shade against your neck, making it appear distorted but beautiful at the same time."

Wow. Suddenly, as he stared at her, she couldn't breathe. Their eyes locked until Gina cleared her throat and abruptly rose. "We need to get back. Poor Dale and Rob must be starving by now." She needed fresh air, as heat had flooded her cheeks.

Stephen nodded, a hint of darkness in his eyes. "I'll get the bill." He turned and walked to the front counter while she got her bearings and climbed down the steps. The soft breeze soothed her flushed cheeks and shivering body. *What the hell?* Why did he have to sound so poetic and sexy? He was deeper than she initially thought. She must have misjudged him.

Her mind not on her actions, she lost her footing and gasped, about to fall forward when two muscular arms held her tight around the waist. She fell back against his chest, closing her eyes briefly until she realised where she was. She moved away from him. "I'm fine. Let's go." Gina walked ahead of him until he reached her side.

"Are you all right?"

"I'm good." She wanted to thank him for saving her back there, but her dried vocal cords prevented that. She had to shake this attraction and not get taken in by his charm, as she knew she'd only be another notch on his belt.

CHAPTER 12

Gina rubbed the back of her neck, her mind flashing back to Stephen and the way she became aroused at his gentle touch around her waist, the way he drew into himself when mentioning his late fiancée, Katie, as if he was still grieving. The pain in his eyes suggested a multitude of layers beneath his outgoing and playful personality. Had she misjudged him?

"Earth to Gina," said Teresa to her as she stared straight ahead at an indigenous painting, while Dalia stood at her side with an arm around her shoulder.

It was Saturday, and they'd decided to visit the city art gallery together. "Sorry, what?" Gina asked. "I'm engrossed in this piece of artwork here. Did you notice that the painter uses a different brush stroke to evoke the darkest of emotions here? Have a look."

Teresa chuckled. "No, I hadn't noticed, but my life just changed."

Dalia shook her head. "What are you thinking about, Gina?" They headed into another room and came across medieval paintings.

Teresa leaned closer to Gina. "She is thinking about Stephen, our client from the health group. They had a pleasant lunch in Geelong two days ago."

Gina flinched. "I am doing no such thing. The man is...is... Oh, never mind. Let's admire this art so I can be inspired for my next piece." A voice behind her made her jolt. She knew that voice.

Stephen approached. "Next piece?"

Teresa looked at her strangely. "Sorry, darl." She frowned. "I might have mentioned we'd be here on Saturday after Stephen explained how he loves art too."

Gina had no words, but her face must have turned as red as a beetroot. The heat in her body increased tenfold. Stephen stood with his arms crossed at his waist and turned to admire the painting opposite.

Dalia squeezed her shoulder and said. "Hi. Stephen, isn't it?" He nodded.

Gina's throat constricted. "Dalia, Stephen is the owner of *Katie's Health Group*. We're marketing his health centres."

Stephen put out his hand. "Great to see you again, Dalia. You must love art as much as Gina does."

She nodded. "I do, but I know little about it. Gina here is the expert."

Gina's legs weighed her down. "Why are you here?"

Stephen curled a brow. "When Teresa mentioned you'd be here on Saturday, I thought you might show me the artists you like so I might be inspired. I, too, come here to brainstorm, develop new ideas for programs." He smirked.

Gina's cheeks warmed. "I am sure you can find your own artists. You seem to know a lot about art and paintings. You don't need my help."

Teresa waved a hand. "Actually, Dalia and I planned to see an exhibition upstairs. We can meet you both later, in, say, an hour?"

Gina glared at her friend. "I'm sure Stephen has other plans and might want to be free to look for himself."

He gave her a cheeky smile. "Not really. No plans, and I could benefit from your expertise." He stood inches from her, her senses sharpened by his citrus cologne. His eyes penetrated hers as he glanced at her lips.

She didn't want to seem rude, so she relented. "Fine, ladies. We will meet you in an hour and not a minute later."

Her friends moved ahead while she squared her shoulders and scrutinised the painting on display.

"Tell me about this painting," he said.

Gina huffed. "The light and shade show the contrast between the hectic pace of the city and the urban space, which is about the lightness of freedom, joy, colour, and vibrancy."

"Hmm. Interesting." He stayed beside her as they walked around viewing the paintings. She struggled to focus when he stood close. His proximity unnerved her, and her hands sweated.

"You know, I enjoy solving puzzles, and you, Gina, are a puzzle. The specks of paint on your two middle fingers, your knowledge of art, and how I overheard you mention 'getting inspired for your next piece'. You're an artist, aren't you?"

Gina gasped, not wanting to share that part of herself. He was getting too personal, and she wanted to keep things strictly professional with him. She ignored him and moved to another painting, not knowing what to say. "This piece is beautiful. Notice the light reflecting against this backdrop, the brushstrokes that form a range of perspectives. What do you think?"

He chuckled as he made his way closer, and then watched her with curiosity. "Great. Now answer my question, Gina."

She turned to him. "Yes, I am. Moving on."

He scurried to keep up with her as she circled the space and then moved into the next room, which featured abstracts. "Wait. Don't run away. You say I'm being childish, but this is the embodiment of childish. Why don't you want me to know? I love that you have a creative side. You have a lot of talents. There's no shame in that."

How could Gina explain that though she hated failure, in her art, she had felt frozen and unable to put herself out there again? She had done it once: she'd asked for a few pieces of her art to be displayed in a gallery, but her art wasn't up to par, and it broke her heart into tiny fragments. How could she deal with rejection again? If someone guaranteed her work would be displayed, she would waste no time in getting it out there. "I don't have shame. It's a part of me I keep private because it gives me order and helps make sense of this screwed up world." He nodded, remaining silent, as if encouraging her to go on. She looked up at the distorted view of a landscape and immersed herself in the painting.

Creating art gave her a sense of control, and space to follow her heart without anyone else telling her how to do it. It was her private, creative arena. "I put myself into my landscape painting as if I can magically transport to a Utopian world, as if I can put my problems aside and forget the past. Forget this...this..." What was she doing? "Oh, never mind. Let's keep going."

Gina retrieved a notebook from her handbag and took notes of the details in one of the Australian coastal regions in an artwork so that it could inspire her for her next painting. She never dared look back at Stephen, whose eyes followed her. She could feel his intense scrutiny, even though she appeared to have silenced him. Was he affected by what she'd said? Had she shown a tad too much vulnerability when she had to keep her distance?

CHAPTER 13

S tephen loved the way Gina walked in her soft sandals as she made her way to the foyer of the museum. Her eyes scanned the space, but her friends had disappeared. He watched her from afar, curious, and found her to be an anomaly. What had she been thinking when she'd stormed out of the room after he'd asked about her artistry? No shame in having creative talent, but she had closed up. What demons haunted her?

His logical mind told him to stay away, but his heart drew him closer to her. When they finally spotted Teresa and Dalia, she ran up to them as if she couldn't get away from him fast enough.

"Hey, Gina. Are you about ready?" asked Dalia.

She nodded. "If you're both leaving, then I'm ready to go too. I'm done here."

He pushed through the crowds walking inside the foyer as he exited with the women, and felt the rush of wind outside Federation Square, the smells of meat and coffee permeating his senses.

Stephen walked beside Gina as he nodded in Teresa's direction. "I'm heading out too. Do you ladies need a lift?"

Teresa shook her head. "No, Dalia's parked on Flinders Street. Where did you park?"

"I've parked down Russel Street. Only a short walk away."

Gina waved to him. "I'll see you during the week, Stephen."

The day was young, and he didn't want it to end. Could he connect with her without scaring her off? If he were to tread cautiously, she might not run a mile and detach herself as she was doing now. He felt as if he couldn't let her get away when he was getting to know her, beginning to have feelings he didn't want. But no harm in enjoying each other's company. It didn't have to be more than that. He'd had enough of challenging women. "Why don't we grab lunch?"

She hesitated, then shook her head. "No, I have work to do at home. Some reports I need to get ready by Monday. It's important for the next step in the marketing campaign."

He waved a hand. "Don't be silly. I don't mind if you're a day late. It's not going to break the bank. Take a bit of time to enjoy your Saturday."

She crossed her arms over her waist. "Don't you have multiple businesses to run? Shouldn't you be working?"

Teresa touched her on the shoulder. "Why don't you enjoy your day? Dalia and I have family commitments. I'll see you on Monday, love."

Dalia nodded. "Yes, go out with Stephen. Enjoy the nice day. Luca and I are visiting his parents. His ever-challenging father."

Gina laughed. "Good luck with that."

He yearned to get to know her and wouldn't let her stubbornness stop him. "No harm in lunch as two professionals being inspired by ideas."

Gina huffed. "Fine. I'll see you both soon." Her friends kissed her goodbye and waved to Stephen. Dalia grinned cheekily as she rushed off towards Teresa.

Gina angled her head. "Let's head off then."

He thought about an upcoming project, and today was the perfect day. Would she agree, or was it a stretch? "I just had an idea." She frowned slightly. "Let's go for a quick trip to the Macedon Ranges. I'm thinking of opening a new centre around there and would love your opinion on the location. What do you think?"

She stiffened. "You do not need me to decide on the location of another centre."

"I would appreciate your opinion, Gina. Come on, take a break. A quick road trip won't kill you and I promise to only talk about work. Nothing else. Nothing personal, as I know you like your privacy. I respect that."

She widened her mouth stretched into a half-smile. "I don't know. I'm not wearing the right clothes, and I don't like long drives. There is so much to plan, and I hate the pressure of last-minute changes. Please go without me."

He didn't want to pressure her, but he had one last card to play. "It could be a chance to get some great pictures for your artwork. How often do you travel to rural Victoria?"

Something shifted in her eyes as she gazed past him. "All right. But you'll need to drop me off at home so I can get a few supplies and other things."

His heart wanted to leap out of his chest. "Of course." He had won this round, but would he next time?

Gina gazed through the window, her back pressed hard against the passenger seat while Stephen raced down the

Calder Freeway like a maniac, zipping in and out of lanes and cutting close to other speeding cars. What was his damn rush?

Her chest was about to pop out of her chest at the vibration of the tiny bumps on the road, and she gasped when a car behind him beeped at being cut off. She shook her head and took calming breaths, closing her eyes to imagine being immersed into one of her abstract paintings.

When he finally made his exit towards Woodend and slowed down, she could breathe freely. He turned to her. "Are you all right?"

She sighed heavily. "I cannot believe how fast you drive. I thought we were going to die, Stephen. The accident we could have had and the drivers beeping you along the way. I am going to drive when we stop next."

"Uh no. Nobody touches my brand-new baby. No one. This is for me only."

She swallowed as he swerved hard around a corner of the country road. "Then I am happy to take an Uber back. Do you know the statistics for drivers with big egos?"

He chuckled. "Jesus, woman. Do you ever let up? Is there ever anything positive you might say? Anything?"

She shifted her body to the window, ignoring him. If he wanted to be rude, she'd avoid talking to him. Why had she agreed to come on this road trip with him? He was a child in a man's body.

The silence was unnerving as Stephen respected her space. At least he knew when he'd lost the battle. Why did he need to speed like he couldn't get there fast enough?

Taking a left turn towards the Hanging Rock Café, she angled her head. "I thought we were heading to a real estate agent about properties in the Macedon Ranges. Why are you going this way?"

"We need to eat first, while we wait for the agent. I'm meeting him in a few hours in Mount Macedon. In the meantime, he's given me a few places to browse. We have time."

Stephen pulled into the parking area and narrowly avoided a woman who rushed past without looking. "Christ." He sighed. "That was not my fault."

Gina nodded. "I hate driving sometimes. You come across people with death wishes, crazy drivers who believe they own the road, and ones who don't follow the rules. It's exhausting to battle the road every day."

Stephen turned off the motor and clasped his hands in his lap, squinting in the bright sunshine. "Let's make a deal."

"What?"

I'd like to see if you can only focus on good things today. Get rid of your negative outlook. Let's see if you can do that for one day."

She scoffed. "Ridiculous. The world is the way it is. Nothing great about it."

Stephen opened the door, and she followed behind until he slowed down and walked beside her, heading down the path towards the café. He stopped her in her tracks by placing his hands on her shoulders and locking eyes with her. The touch of his firm hands on her shoulders rendered her speechless, a spine-tingling sensation that made her dizzy breathing in his heady peppermint scent. "How about you see this as a challenge, or as something you can achieve? I know you thrive on those, so for today, just see the good things. For example, the sweeping tree-lined path or the laughing crowds. Only for today. How about it?"

Gina wasn't one to refuse a battle. Game on. "Fine. I can do that for one day. Not a problem." When he took his hands off her shoulders, he cleared his throat and walked ahead. The warmth of his hands continued to radiate throughout her body.

CHAPTER 14

G ina sat on a hard chair outside the café, looking out over the spacious reserve across from the Hanging Rock café. Towering trees in the distance surrounded the bushland and lined up haphazardly. Children kicked a soccer ball near the barbecue facilities, where loose logs, twigs, and sticks lay amidst flat, dry, green grass. Passersby strolled through the reserve and along paths, heading down to the Discovery Centre, which housed the history and the recorded incidences of Hanging Rock.

The young waitress smiled on approach, and they ordered a chicken burger for Stephen and minestrone soup for Gina. A whiff of her floral perfume permeated the air as tables filled up. A wave of heat washed over the back of her neck, her hands sweating despite the mild temperature of the building. Why was she nervous?

Stephen eyed her curiously. "I like the cosiness of this place, don't you?"

She nodded. "It's quaint and brings back memories of when I came here with my family. That was a long time ago now." She shifted. "It's been a while since we did something fun. I miss those times."

"Tell me about your family," Stephen said.

She could've kicked herself for bringing up her family when it involved her sister, and that was a topic she refused to discuss. "My parents are amazing. They instilled in me a strong work ethic, but my father was strict. If I didn't get top marks on my exams or assignments, he'd push me to do better next time."

"That must have been a lot of pressure on you."

She shrugged. "Yes, but it also pushed me to excel, made sure I did everything right, and never swayed from the rules. A few people I knew would cheat on their exams, but they never got away with it."

He teased. "I never would have guessed you had that kind of ambition or always did things the right way. Have you ever broken a rule in your life?"

She shook her head. "Funny, Stephen, but yes, I have. Rare, but I have."

Stephen leaned forward, raising an eyebrow. "Do you have any brothers or sisters?"

Gina swallowed, averting her eyes. "A sister, Toni." She had no energy to talk about her today. "What about your family?"

The waitress approached with their food and drinks. A glass of Riesling for her and a beer for him.

The scent of herbs from the soup and the saltiness of the chips incited her hunger. She yearned to grab one, but held back.

"Here, have a chip before I devour them all," Stephen said.

She forced a smile, then grabbed a chip, chewing and savouring the soft, salty texture while Stephen's gaze lingered on her lips. It was damn sexy until she looked away.

She sipped her wine, then picked up her spoon to taste the tender vegetables and pepper, which left a lasting impression on her tongue. The heat burned her lips, so she winced while Stephen devoured his chicken burger, squeezing the roll as sauce dripped down his chin. He licked his lips, and Gina held the spoon in mid-air, frozen to the core as her knees loosened and parted slightly. *What the hell?* What would it feel like to taste those lips or have his tongue glide down the middle of her chest? *No.*

"Anyway, about my family. I've got two younger brothers, and parents who are still as much in love as they were over thirty-five years ago. They've always instilled in me a strong work ethic and good values. My father's a jokester and my mother's the more responsible of the two, but opposites attract, don't you think?"

Gina averted her eyes and ignored the question. "They sound lovely. Are you close to your brothers?"

He nodded. "I am, but we don't get to see each other often because of our busy jobs and their marriages. One of them has a young daughter, but I get to see them when I can. We keep in regular phone contact."

Gina swallowed more soup, then put the spoon down slowly. She hardly knew the man and didn't like how personal this was getting. She tapped her foot, deciding to change the subject. "I am sure you know about the missing girls at Hanging Rock."

Stephen gave her a strange look, no doubt wondering why she'd changed the topic so abruptly. "Common knowledge,' he said, while chewing on another chip. "Sad story."

She sighed. "The private girls' school was never the same after those four people went missing, including their teacher."

He placed a finger on his temple. "I can imagine. Never knowing what happened to them. No sense of closure."

"One of the girls returned, but she had no memory of the Rock. After several months, there was this energy that stayed around the school and led to students becoming sombre, and many of the staff members resigning. One girl fell to her death and the headmistress killed herself by jumping off Hanging Rock. The school was never the same. I watched the movie but so desperately wanted to know the mystery. It's frustrating not to know."

"Wasn't that at the start of the twentieth century? If it happened now, we'd have a lot more resources to find them. More sophisticated investigation techniques. But what made you think about that story?"

Gina leaned forward. "Just that we're at Hanging Rock and I love historical facts. I don't love unsolved mysteries."

Stephen wiped his mouth with the napkin, tilting his head as if curious. "I can see that about you, but not all mysteries can be solved." He took a breath. "I listened to this one crime podcast that infuriated me when the crimes went unsolved, so I stopped listening. I love figuring things out, but you can't always get what you want. Life's not that simple."

"Aren't you an impulsive guy who wants immediate gratification?"

He shook his head. "Hell no. I am more patient than you think. But speaking of mysteries, I could do a whole marathon watching crime and thriller movies."

"I probably could too. I love thrillers and psychological suspense with twists and surprises you never see coming."

"Which movies do you like?"

She swallowed more soup before replying. "Shutter Island, The Sixth Sense—a classic—Gone Girl, just to name a few. Even those about real life serial killers like Ted Bundy and Jeffrey Dahmer are intriguing. I hate the gore and violence though. It's the suspense and puzzles to solve that keep me watching."

"Shutter Island was great, but too long, and Sixth Sense had a great twist." He exhaled. "You seem to love a good scare."

"I do, but I'm not fond of action-adventure because they're usually too violent and bloody.' She envisioned what it would feel like to have him close to her on her couch as they watched these movies.

He chewed the last of his burger. "The bloodier the better I say, but each to their own. I know men are wired to be hardened and gritty, while women generally want soft and nurturing," he said with a cocky grin.

She shook her head. "That is sexist. I don't do nurturing or soft, so do not put me in that box. If I got soft that way,

I would never have achieved what I have. I wouldn't let emotions get in my way."

"Right, so you're saying you don't have emotions? We all need them."

"Emotions get in the way of everything, and I much prefer to see things as black and white, so they make sense. Emotions make little sense. They're irrational."

"But you're a painter. That's emotions right there."

She shrugged. "That's different. It's my private space where I can be free to create without having to publicly express what I feel."

He nodded. "Right. Maybe you prefer expressing yourself privately, but I'm sure you would've been emotional in past relationships."

How did they end up here? "Not that it did me any good. I had to learn the hard way."

Stephen scanned her from eyes to lips, and it caused a flutter in her heart. "Tell me about the creep who hurt you. I'd be happy to beat him up for you."

She laughed but didn't feel like sharing the tale of her ex-boyfriend, who no longer deserved her attention. Even her so-called sister didn't deserve her energy. "I would rather not share."

He leaned forward and smacked his lips together, examining her. "If I share, will you?"

She had nothing to lose considering that they'd no longer see each other after their marketing contract ended. He'd be gone in the ether. "You first then." Gina squared her shoulders. "You mentioned your ex-fiancée. Can you tell me about her?"

Stephen gazed past her, giving an audible sigh, his eyes misty. "Katie was loved by everyone. She put others' needs before her own. Gave her all." He took another breath. "She was working non-stop when she partnered with me in the business. She was born in New Zealand and wanted to open up a centre there. She missed her home, but having a health centre in her native country would've given her the chance to visit often." He clenched his hands. "She ignored my pleas to slow down and delegate more of her tasks. She was an achiever, like you, Gina. Had ambitions."

Gina's heart ached for him, wishing the pain in his eyes didn't hit her like a ton of bricks. "She sounds amazing."

"She was." He swallowed and scratched the inside of his palm. "I forced her to see the doctor after she'd complained of chest pains. The doctor assessed her pain, prescribed painkillers, and referred her for tests and to a cardiologist."

"Sounds like a caring doctor," Gina said.

"She was, but Katie always came up with an excuse about not having time to follow up on tests, and said she stopped having chest pain. But the doctor believed she had a cardiac issue. I was worried, but Katie was stubborn."

"What happened next?"

Stephen focused on her, hesitating. "I drove to her place one night when she was preparing dinner in the kitchen. I was in the living room when I heard a noise. A plate shattered. I went to the kitchen and found her lying on the floor, writhing in pain. She was having a heart attack. I called 000 and they explained what to do. The aspirin didn't help, and when she stopped breathing, I did CPR...but it was too late. The heart attack was too severe."

Gina reached for his hand, a tightness in her chest. "I am so sorry. I cannot imagine how traumatic that must have been for you."

He bit down on his bottom lip. "If only I'd pushed her harder to get help. If only I got her admitted into hospital. If only I had got to her sooner and forced her to take her medication. She'd been skipping it."

She shook her head. "You did everything you possibly could, Stephen. Sometimes no matter what we do, it's never enough. A lot of things are out of our control."

He angled his head. "I am better off alone. No pain. Easier that way."

Time passed by awkwardly as they sat in silence while they finished their lunch. Stephen got up as if he hadn't just spilled such an emotional story. "Ready to go to the health centre?"

"Sure." Gina tried to ignore the deep, empty pit in her stomach, shaking off her desire to protect him. The trauma he'd suffered was unimaginable. Was she beginning to care for him more than she wanted?

CHAPTER 15

Stephen surveyed the wide, open space in the town of Mount Macedon, enjoying the scents of pine, freshly cut grass, and blossoms around the grand colonial home. The path was bordered by land that had a gentle incline and hedges. A scattering of trees bunched around gave it a rural ambiance.

He walked uphill towards the steps to the cream façade and admired the colonial windows, the balustrades running down the side of the house, with a small round table and two cane chairs by the front door.

The real estate agent, Tim, was a stocky man with a long beard and beady eyes. He stopped at the top of the steps and waved his hands around while Gina glanced briefly in his direction, her eyes shining, no doubt due to the beauty of the countryside. "This lodge is known as one of the area's premier estates. It has been restored and is within three hectares of the amazing botanical gardens. It features a gazebo, grass tennis courts, a four-bedroom cottage, and a pool."

"This is so beautiful," said Gina, briefly turning to Stephen. "See? A positive statement. I can do it."

Stephen chuckled while the agent angled his head and pushed open the door to the home. "An inside joke," he explained to the man.

The massive living area featured amazing views of the mountains and landscape outside, with white-washed wall to wall open-plan living and brown glossy flooring.

Tim beamed in their direction as he walked around the room. "As you can see, the home offers brilliant garden views. We have rich timber walls, ceiling panels, and a stone fireplace that provides an historic yet cosy space over the well-measured formal rooms. The design was meant to satisfy both family dining and elaborate functions." He waved another arm around. "The kitchen features stone benches and a fully equipped pantry. You get natural light through floor to ceiling glass coming in. There's also a picturesque pool and a nearby barbecue terrace."

The man droned on, but Stephen had lost track of what he was saying as he watched Gina unbutton the top of her blouse. A redness on her skin flashed across the centre of her chest. The way her t-shirt hugged her feminine curves made him desire her, curious as to how she would feel against a plush rug opposite the fireplace. He'd explore her body with his hungry lips and make her scream his name. *Stop!*

"I will give you two time to explore and return within an hour."

Stephen nodded. "Thanks, Tim."

Gina's head turned in every direction until she approached the window and stared outside. "What are your plans for this place? It is so grand."

He enjoyed the warmth of the sunlight but it made him squint. "I'd like to use this as a health retreat for preventative healthcare, and cater to those with chronic health conditions. A home away from home."

Gina made her way to one of the spacious bedrooms and he followed her, but she remained silent until reaching the bathroom that was like a little house on its own. It had a marble bathtub, marble counters, and two windows offering light and a view of the plants outside.

He drew closer to her and accidentally bumped into her, the heat in his loins rendering him almost speechless. "Sorry."

She inched back, her eyes darting again through the window with its venetian blinds. "I can give you the demographics of Mount Macedon, based on 2021 statistics." He arched a brow and waited, knowing she loved her research and facts. "The average age is forty-eight, with slightly more males than females living here. Most are married and have a degree or higher education. Most of them are full-time professional employees, with a small unemployed population." He was entranced by her memory of all that, yearning to reach out and brush aside a strand of hair from across her eye. "Most of those who live here are Australian born." She paused. "You can offer walking tours, hydrotherapy in the pool outside, and tennis for those who are fit. Assuming most are financially able, you could offer services at an affordable price to get repeat business."

"Wow. When did you find the time to research the demographics?"

"While you were driving here," she said.

"And you remembered all that?"

Gina shrugged before making her way back to the lounge area and pulling open the glass door that led to the cottage and swimming pool. She turned to him. "I love facts, and I have an amazing memory, Stephen." Her eyes scanned the area. "You could do so much here."

He loved how her eyes lit up. "Yes, I plan to run yoga and meditation classes, as well as remedial and relaxation massages. Possibly even osteopathy or myotherapy."

"The cost to not only buy this outright but to maintain it will be astronomical. Are you sure about this?"

He admired her perceptiveness. "Definitely, and funds are not a problem. My other businesses pay for themselves, and I can see this as a potential success. Obviously, it won't be ready for a long time yet, but in stages, we'll get there."

"It's impressive how many businesses you own."

He stared past her. "With improvement in business, I'll be worry-free. Almost. The nightclub doesn't need much from me. This health retreat and the new centre in New Zealand will be my next projects. I would love to aim for global expansion, but I'm still young, so who knows what I can achieve."

"But all that responsibility. Doesn't it get exhausting?"

He shook his head. "I love keeping busy as it keeps me sane. I thrive on distractions and creative ventures." A fleeting darkness filled his heart as he refused to think about future relationships. Surely, he could thrive on business alone.

After spending time near the pool, they made their way around to more bedrooms and another two bathrooms, until finally reaching a deck and terrace with peaceful garden views that featured rosebushes, orchids, low brush, and hedges around plant beds. He could adapt to this, but he knew he'd soon get bored without the hustle and bustle of the city.

"I admire your dedication to helping others," said Gina.

He frowned. "A compliment. I never would've expected that from you."

A fleeting cheeky grin lit up her face. "I am full of mystery; don't you know that?" She made her way to a freestanding building that overlooked topiary gardens. The gentle breeze caressed her glossy hair in the sunlight as she crossed her arms over her waist and peered out into the mountainous landscape. "Will you buy it?"

"I sure will. I can target the locals and tourists to the area, and with this space, I can have a few guests stay at the same time. They'd all need to be vetted, of course."

Stomping footsteps behind them made Stephen turn around. "You're back."

Tim nodded. "Yes. What are your thoughts about this beautiful garden estate? Has it won you over?"

Stephen beamed. "Absolutely. Hand me the papers and I'll get my solicitor on to it straight away. This is the perfect space for what I have in mind. Thank you."

Tim's eyes lit up as he patted his briefcase. "I have it all in here. Let's move to the kitchen and I'll explain the contract and terms."

Stephen locked eyes with Gina, whose softened gaze endeared him to her, but he was curious as to whether she'd still be around once this house was ready for business.

CHAPTER 16

Inside her home the following evening, Gina set the mug of coffee down on the glass table opposite Dalia and shook her head. The steam from the beverage gave her a small distraction from her friend's comment. "There is no way I like the man. He is not my type and can be pompous. He is convinced he can own the world. Too carefree for my liking. Since when do I go for men like that? My complete opposite?"

Dalia chuckled. "Right. Sure, you don't like him. But opposites do attract, just like Luca and me. If we didn't appreciate our differences, we wouldn't have realised we have a lot in common too."

Gina dragged her coffee closer and wrapped her hands around the mug. "We might have a few things in common, but it doesn't mean anything. We're tolerating each other, and he might have a few layers I didn't see at first, but still. We get along as professionals, nothing more."

"Really? If you say so, Gina."

Gina found it unbelievable they were discussing a man who would never be considered seriously by her. She might have had a fun time with him, but that was all it was. He might make her heart flutter, but it was only because he was different and intriguing.

"Okay, so he has given us business and I appreciate his company for doing that, but after we are done, we are done. I won't see him again and we'll go our separate ways." A rush of cold swam into her stomach. "Can we talk about something else, please? Have you heard from Rose?"

Dalia sipped the remainder of her coffee. "She called the other day when you were in Geelong, and is thriving with the retreat. All foreigners who don't mind spending money. Some of them have even returned for more writing inspiration."

Gina nodded. "I am so excited for her. Who would have thought she'd have her own business, apart from her author business? I do miss her."

"Me too, but I have a feeling she might be visiting in a few months. We'll see."

When her phone buzzed on the kitchen counter, she got up and checked the display. *Stephen.* Butterflies swam in Gina's stomach. "Hi Stephen. This is a surprise."

"Hi Gina. I've booked the tickets to New Zealand for those dates you gave me. We're leaving in a week. I'll text you the details."

Gina swallowed, wondering what she'd got herself into. But her boss was adamant she handle this campaign too. It was only part of her job, and she thrived on giving the best version of herself in business. "Thanks for sharing that with me. I will start getting ready."

"Great. I'll be seeing you."

Gina ended the call, and the look on Dalia's face was priceless. Her friend's sassy, broad grin made her sick to the stomach. The idea of her spending even more time with a man she was attracted to was gut-wrenching. But she refused to get attached.

Stephen put away his phone. He lay against the sofa pillow with his legs up on the footrest, his eyes scanning a sports update on TV, but not truly taking it in. Dale held a can of beer in his hand and looked at him strangely.

"You have it bad," Dale said.

Stephen winced. "What are you talking about?"

"The way your eyes lit up during the call. How you seemed to be in your own world, like you are smitten. Are you?"

He shook his head. "Are you mad? She is a beautiful woman, but we're only friends, or at least, I hope we are. She might tell you a different story because of her pride, but we got closer in Mount Macedon. At least we're not fighting anymore."

"I know you, Stephen. Be honest. How do you truly feel about her?"

Stephen wanted to say that he couldn't stop thinking about her day and night, couldn't stop dreaming about her, couldn't stop seeing the way her eyes softened when speaking about her friends. He tried distracting himself, but the more he got to know her, the more he wanted to see her. But he couldn't take that risk. "There might be an attraction, but I am not going there. I can't dishonour Katie either, nor go through that pain again."

Dale sighed and set his can on the glass coffee table. "I get it man, but you wouldn't be dishonouring Katie. She'd want you to be happy."

He shook his head. "I am happy the way I am, Dale. Keeping things light with Gina is how it needs to be." Stephen realised that the last time they had lunch in

Woodend, she had avoided talking about her sister. Were they not close?

"It was hard for me to give Cammie her freedom after she got sick, but after a time, I adapted, and now she's fully recovered. You don't know how things will pan out if you don't take a chance and learn to trust. There are no guarantees in anything, but that doesn't mean you stop living."

"Sure, but Cammie's alive and Katie's not. I can't risk that pain again, Dale. Different situation."

His friend picked up the remote and switched channels to a sports program. "Think about it, Stephen. Don't rule Gina out."

"Whatever, Dale."

Stephen wished he could open himself up more, but he didn't want to face any more pain than he had to. He knew Gina was all around negative in her perspective, but over the past few weeks, he found a slight change. She was becoming more positive about life, and he hoped it was due to his influence. But that was all it was. Friendship. He didn't want to ruin that, and a part of him wondered if it was a great idea to travel to New Zealand with her, even though she'd be an asset to his new business venture. "How about we watch the game and put women on the back burner for now?"

"Sure. Not a problem. But I still say to take a chance. She could be the one." He stroked his chin. "I have a question for you. Gina's a beautiful woman and you'd easily consider a fling with any attractive female, so why haven't you had a fling with Gina, without getting attached?"

He shifted his legs and closed his eyes, wondering, if he and Gina didn't have a professional relationship, would he have jumped in bed with her? Why hadn't he even propositioned her for a fling without strings?

CHAPTER 17

G ina's breathing increased as her eyes stared past the pilot, Jerry, a thin middle-aged man with a paunch. The swoosh of the Essendon airfield as other small planes took off gave her an earache. What was she doing here? Couldn't they go to a normal airport like normal people?

Stephen scrutinised her before facing the pilot. "Jerry here can reassure you about the safety of the Cessna. Hear him out."

Jerry rubbed his hands together and gave her a reassuring grin. It did nothing to ease the constriction in her chest or the ache in her shoulders. "Okay, Ms Cassani. I can assure you that the Cessna has flown since 1955 and has had some upgrades. I can tell you it's quite safe and I am an experienced pilot with over twenty years of flying mileage. You are in safe hands, Ms Cassani."

She nodded. "Yes, I know. I read about Timm and Cook setting the world record from December 4, 1958, to February 7, 1959, for flight endurance. They took off from the International Airport in Las Vegas, Nevada, and landed back at the airport after sixty-four days in a flight that spanned an estimated 150,000 miles. The flight was part of a fund-raising effort for the Damon Runyon Cancer Fund. I know the aircraft is now on display at the airport. I understand it is safe, but tell that to my body."

Stephen chuckled at the dilation in the pilot's eyes. "I know. She loves her facts." He squeezed her shoulder, and her breathing calmed a tad. "It is perfectly safe and only takes about three and a half hours to get to New Zealand. You will blink and we'll be there."

Ignoring the trembling of her bottom lip, she squared her shoulders. "Let's get it over with." The air felt thick as Stephen prodded her, her heavy legs carrying her forward. She squeezed into the rear of the plane.

Stephen sat next to her and gave her headphones. "Here. Wear these." She put them over her head and waited for the pilot to prepare for take-off. "Relax, Gina. You'll be fine. We can talk about any topic of your choice to make this trip seem faster." His smile widened, causing her heart to tingle. "The Cessna has been around for a long time, and it's not only popular but the most successful plane in history."

She clasped her hands. "I hear you, but like I said earlier, tell that to my body."

Stephen put on his headphones as the pilot prepared for their departure, then cleared his throat as he glanced at her lips as if he wanted to say something. Why did she have to refer to her body again? She was obviously not thinking straight when she wanted to do all kinds of things to Stephen's body. *Hell!* Why did he make her heart clench with the way he licked his lips, focussed straight ahead with his skin-tight jeans and a figure-hugging t-shirt? Even his fresh-smelling citrus cologne drew her in further.

After take-off, they flew in silence as the whirring sound of the wings accelerated her heartbeat, but she put on a happy face, not wanting him to see her as weak and fragile. She could do this.

As the plane reached altitude, Gina gazed through the window and fought against her flipping stomach, taking in the green and beige landscape, the small river, and minute houses. A warmth enveloped her hand and she realised that Stephen had gently picked it up to reassure her with his touch. The firmness and heat in his palms made her feel something unfamiliar and scary until she moved her hand away. She wouldn't get sucked in by his charms.

Calm breathing and closed eyes helped her visualise a safe space of being on solid ground, but the voice beside her broke her reverie. She turned. "What did you say?"

"I said, are you all right?"

Resting a hand against her heart, she said, "I will be once we land. I feel as if the plane's about to throw us into the air without protection. The turbulence is madness, and the deafening sound might lead to me buying hearing aids. I assume you travel often?"

He nodded. "For my businesses, investors, that sort of thing. I absolutely love the way I feel on the light plane. The easy flow, the lightness, the poof of air as you take off, the air pressure, and the amazing views. I must admit it was hard the first time, but it gets easier. You come to appreciate the vastness of this world. How there's something bigger than ourselves. Something magical. I can't explain the way I feel up here, but it's an adrenaline rush."

Gina chuckled. "I should have known you'd use those words. Don't you ever like security, stability, and knowing exactly what's going to happen every day?"

He sighed. "Of course. When the situation calls for it. But the unknown is what makes life fun and exciting. I love challenges, and with routine, you get hardly any of that."

Gina started to wonder if she was too boring in wanting things to stay the same. But no, she was responsible. He might have had a good head for business, but he would only end up hurting her in the end. She had to stay focussed and not get taken in by his fully kissable lips, his broad physique, or the glossy blonde streaks in his hair.

With views of sandy beaches, a waterfront promenade, and surrounding hills increasing as the plane descended several hours later, her stomach somersaulted. Houses around the surrounding hills and the harbour took her breath away, but as the Cessna flew lower, with bunched up trees surrounding her, the plane glided in between greenery over a river with the backdrop of sunlit mountains in the distance, featuring hues of browns, greens, and yellows. The closeness made her breath stop as she clenched her hands and gritted her teeth.

Gina's stomach flipped as she imagined the plane submerging into the river below, despite knowing the pilot's experience. The breathtaking view offered solace as she turned to glance at Stephen, who gave her a reassuring smile.

"Don't worry. Jerry's got this," he said.

Those words gave her reassurance and spread warmth in her chest. Who would have thought he'd make her feel safe?

The plane descended and steered towards an embankment around a corner, past the river and body of water trails to a rough landing on a flat airstrip. Gina closed her eyes tight and felt the soothing squeeze of Stephen's hand on hers. The loud screech of the brakes made her wince and her body shifted from side to side. She breathed a sigh of relief as it slowed down and stopped completely. They had reached New Zealand.

"Welcome to Wellington," said Jerry.

Gina faced her companion with the widest grin. What a relief.

Later that evening, Stephen glanced across at his companion with sweaty palms, heavy breathing, and an image of his lips gliding across her chest. Why did she look so much more attractive with less make-up? Au natural. She would drive him crazy tonight knowing she'd be sleeping in the hotel room next door.

He sat at a wide desk in his hotel room with papers spread out. Taking a deep breath, he concentrated and got on with business.

Gina picked up a document outlining the financials of the business he'd be taking over. "The health centre hasn't done too badly in terms of profits but still not enough to cover expenses. Do you think you can turn that around?"

He shrugged. "It's why you're here with me. The manager's having second thoughts about selling his business to me. If you explain your marketing tactics, projections, and future growth, we can show him it'll grow under my ownership. But this trip could be a waste of time," he lied. Seeing her away from everyone and everything else gave him the chance to get to know her, despite a part of him knowing it was a bad idea to get involved. But he couldn't control his heart. "I can discuss my credentials and plans to expand, but it depends on what the others have to offer." He leaned forward and his leg grazed hers. She quickly shifted back in her chair. "I have faith in you, which is why I'll let you start the conversation."

Her shoulders lifted and a warm, fuzzy feeling in her stomach made her smile. Did Stephen truly believe in her? "Okay, but it's all about the demographics. They need more visibility around the untapped markets." She picked up the business's prospectus. "Pilates and osteopathy can be lucrative. But let's put emphasis on the prevention of chronic disease."

He got up. "Would you like a coffee before we head out? We've still got an hour. Let's chill."

She chuckled. "That can't be hard for you." She crossed one leg over another, and he couldn't help but stare at her bare thigh underneath the black skirt. *Holy hell.* He was getting hard, so he turned around before she noticed.

He got two cups started with sugar and spilled a heap over the floor. Gina got up and grabbed a cloth then scooped it up. He moved to pick up the remainder with a paper towel when she toppled and lost her balance, about to fall back. Stephen dropped his sugar and held on to her, holding her still. Their eyes locked, his heart beating a mile a minute while Gina leaned in and licked her lips. Stephen moved in within inches of her as he ran his fingers across her jawline. She closed her eyes and parted her lips, but when she opened them and his lips reached closer, Gina moved away.

"I think I will...aah...skip the coffee. I'd like to freshen up in my room. How about I see you in the foyer in an hour?"

Stephen hid his disappointment. "Oh, right, of course." She retrieved her bag without looking at him and closed the door behind her. What had just happened? They were so close to kissing. But he had to respect her wishes. Did she not care about him as much as he cared about her? Had he misread the signs?

CHAPTER 18

S tephen sat opposite Gina in a fine dining restaurant. She wore a slimming black dress with a low neckline that showed cleavage, dangly pearl earrings, a black shawl around her toned shoulders, and high wedged heels that made her legs go on forever. If only he could stop the lurching of his heart every time he looked at her.

She cut through a small piece of steak and chewed thoughtfully, as if something was on her mind. No doubt their near kiss from earlier that day.

What enticed him was the scent of mint and soap as he drew near to her, the way her lips appeared to be a tad lop-sided when she smiled, the way she looked past him when nervous, and even the way she chewed her lip. She was doing his head in, and he didn't know what to do with these strange feelings.

"Penny for your thoughts," said Gina. "You look miles away."

Stephen forked his creamy chicken and chewed a piece before replying. "I've been thinking about how we've got a chance to purchase this new health centre."

She wiped her mouth with a napkin. "I agree, but you'll need to wait at least two weeks before a response. Patience is a virtue."

He sighed. "I am patient. I was hoping we'd know in a few days. We can't stay here for two weeks."

"Hmm. I admit it would've been easier to sort out the paperwork in person, but you can always fly back here. It's not a long flight."

He chuckled. "Too long for you though. I don't often see you scared of anything. In fact, it's usually the other way around; you scaring everyone else."

The burly male server intervened. "Here is another bottle of wine," he said as he poured it into their wine glasses. "Enjoy."

"Thank you," said Stephen and watched the man walk away. "But I must say you did well, considering your fear on the plane. It must be hard not to be in control."

She pursed her lips. "It is a struggle for me to be without control because I didn't always have that over the years. Life can be crappy sometimes."

He wondered what that meant. Had she experienced trauma or pain in the past? How could he ask without scaring her away? He got the sense that something wasn't right with her sister. "Last time you mentioned having a sister but didn't say much about her."

Gina's face paled as if he'd asked her to have sex right on this table. She touched the centre of her neck, which flushed red. She swallowed a few times while gulping her wine as if it was water. "Nothing to say. We don't see each other much."

He waited for more, but it didn't come, and he didn't want to pressure her. "Speaking of not seeing each other much, at one point, my father had a heart attack. It was a scary time because the doctors weren't sure he was going to make it. It worried me after..."

"After Katie's heart attack?" Gina asked.

"Exactly, but it forced me to let everything go: business, meetings, new investors, all so I could stay with him for a few weeks after he got out of the hospital. I didn't care about work, only my dad. He almost died, but thank God he made it through after surgery, change of diet, medications, and exercise. That was two years ago, and now he's never been healthier."

"That's good to hear. Again, I am sorry about your fiancée."

Stephen nodded. "I'd thought Katie would be okay too, but Dad's heart attack brought it all back." He took a calming breath. A twinge in his chest made him wince. "I wish Katie had slowed down and thought more about her health." He fought back tears. "It's why I want to expand my work and reach more people. Preventative health is so much better for the economy. I can help prevent heart issues."

Gina leaned forward. "I agree, and what you are doing is admirable. Grief is hard. I know."

He angled his head. "I vowed to delegate more of my work and have good people helping me out in all my businesses. Balance is important, which is why I need my playful side—to balance myself out."

"That makes sense," she said. Her phone buzzed in her bag, so she rummaged for it and checked the display. "Sorry. I need to get this."

"Of course." She got up from the table and headed outside into the foyer, her voice a little raised, as if she was upset by something. Gina was a mystery, and he intended to peel away those layers.

When Gina returned, she drank down her remaining wine then lifted a hand.

The server approached. "How can I help?"

"Another bottle please."

"Certainly, madam," he said and ambled away.

"Is everything okay?" asked Stephen.

"Peachy," she said.

Stephen nodded and chewed the remainder of his chicken. But he no longer had an appetite. His heart went out to her as it seemed as if she was going through something. If only he could get her to confide in him, but she sat in silence and cut into her steak, her mind distant.

The server returned and poured wine into her glass then rested the bottle on the table as Stephen's glass was still half full. "Enjoy."

Gina picked up her glass with a shaky hand and drank down half of it then dabbed at her mouth with a napkin.

"Are you sure you're okay?" Stephen asked.

"I need another drink." She filled half of her glass with wine then drank it all down.

Stephen waved a hand. "Take it easy with that wine, Gina. I don't want to carry you out of here. Maybe you should have some water."

"I'm fine," she said. "I don't need you to be my keeper. I'm a grown woman."

"That you are," said Stephen, thinking how much of a beautiful woman she was, and how he couldn't stop thinking about her day and night. His heart broke at seeing her in pain, but she wasn't about to share.

Gina went to grab the bottle again, but Stephen lay a hand over hers. "No more. You've had enough. What if I want more wine?"

"You're not drinking, so I assume you don't."

"Why don't you tell me what's bothering you? I might be able to help."

She scoffed. "Help. The party guy, the bachelor who thinks life is amazing when it isn't. The man who has to buy more businesses just to make himself feel better. That guy." She bowed down. "I'm sorry. That was cruel."

Stephen's chest constricted, but he knew she was partly drunk. But weren't truer words spoken when you drank? "It's fine. What was that phone call about?"

She laughed and threw her head back. "I... My parents had the nerve to tell me my sister's coming down to show off her new boyfriend."

He nodded. "Right. Where does she live?"

"In Perth. She found work there and ended up living in Broome. I was happy not seeing her, but now she has the nerve to ruin my life again. I refuse to see her. She doesn't deserve my time nor energy."

Stephen was curious. "What happened between you two?"

Gina stared into her hands then dug her nails into her palms. "She... She...slept with my ex-boyfriend."

Stephen flinched. His body froze. Had he heard her correctly? "I am so sorry, Gina. I have no words. That's horrible."

Gina shrugged. "It is what it is." She sneered. "I don't trust many people in my life."

He reached for her hand and stroked it. "You can trust me, Gina. Always."

She chuckled. "Right. I don't trust any Stephens, and you're a client."

Something unfamiliar tugged at his heart as he only wanted to protect her and make her feel safe. If he could kiss her pain away, he so desperately wanted to, but she was far too vulnerable, and he wasn't that kind of guy. "Have you spoken to your sister since then?" She shook her head. "Sometimes the grief over losing someone important to you can be worse than their actions. I hated how Katie never listened when I told her to slow down. No doubt the burnout contributed to it. But grief is something you cannot control when the person dies. When it's a lost relationship, it's different. You have control."

Gina raised an eyebrow. "I respect what you went through, Stephen, but she hurt me. What she did was unforgivable. She betrayed me and I'll never get past it."

"I am only suggesting you think about seeing her."

Gina rose from the table and downed more wine. "Sorry. I have to go."

He flailed his hand. "Wait. Please." But before he could stop her, she scurried out of the restaurant without looking back. A pleasant trip away ended up being a disaster and all because he had to push her on it. It was her life, and he had no right to tell her what to do.

CHAPTER 19

Gina's hands turned clammy as she sat inside a shuttle bus for their trip to Queenstown. Stephen didn't say much about their impulsive trip, but she got the sense this boat trip wasn't a slow, relaxed ride. He had apologised for his comment at dinner last night, but she still couldn't believe she'd opened up to him about her sister. She'd obviously had too much to drink and wouldn't make that same mistake again. But at least she had apologised when a sense of guilt crushed her at the way she had spoken to him when he only wanted to help.

Stephen sat beside her as he gazed out the window, his leg brushing hers, sending tingles down her spine.

She shifted closer to the window and faced him. "Why are we going on this boat trip? How did you even hear about it?"

"The manager, Jared, from the health centre recommended it when you were talking to the osteopath at our meeting. I thought, why not? I love fun, and you need more of it, Gina."

She sighed. "I don't know about this, Stephen. How scary is this? You know I prefer to plan things and do them at my pace."

"We're leaving in a couple of days, so I thought we'd see a bit of New Zealand and be adventurous. Remember how I told you to be more positive? Well, this is one way. By being daring and doing something adrenaline-filled with a positive mindset."

She scrolled through her phone. "Oh, my goodness. I don't like the sound of this." She glanced at the website on her display, reading about the driver's fancy moves and tricks. How would she even survive the fast ride?

Stephen glanced at her reassuringly. "Look, you survived the Cessna. This is only on water rather than air, so it's a bit more exciting. You will love it. I've done this before, and it is perfectly safe. The driver's experienced, an expert, so chill."

"Chill?" She scoffed. "I am not happy about this, Stephen. Not happy."

He squeezed her shoulder. "You are totally safe with me. Absolutely safe." Their eyes lingered until she looked past him and remained silent. Why was he trying to change who she was by taking control? She didn't like it, but she wouldn't make a scene with a busload of people surrounding them.

The guide, a stocky man with a beard a mile long said, "We have reached the Shotover River." He recited housekeeping instructions, but Gina tuned out as she felt Stephen's hand brush her thigh. Was it accidental?

Gina gripped her lifejacket as she stood on the shore of the Shotover River while others had already taken their seats on the jet boat, staring and whispering opposite her. The mild wind brushed her heated cheeks, and her body sweated and shivered as if it was chilly in the warm sunshine.

Stephen watched her curiously and took a calming breath. "I'll be right beside you, Gina. The driver knows what he's doing and can manoeuvre his way around the water. Don't worry. I've got you." His gaze ran deep into hers.

The driver showed them a diagram of the boat and recited safety instructions that she barely heard with her chest squeezing tight, as if she was having a panic attack.

Her bottom lip trembled as she imagined all the accidents that had happened on boats in news stories she'd read. What if they hit a large boulder, and the boat capsized? What if the driver lost his grip on the steering wheel? What if he got distracted and flew them all into the air? "Too much can happen."

"What's life without a bit of risk, and this"—he turned and pointed to the boat—"is low risk. I've been on one of these before, and believe me, it is so much fun. Nothing will happen. Like I said, I've got you. Hold on tight to my hand and you'll be fine."

Gina nodded, then recalled a traumatic experience she never thought she'd recover from. If she could survive trauma, she could survive a silly boat ride. "Fine, Stephen."

"That's my girl," he said.

Gina's cheeks warmed as she followed him onto the boat while holding his hand. She took a step down from the plank and boarded, fighting against dizziness and dry throat as she walked over to the padded seating with two spare seats in the middle. Her hands sweated as she calmed her breathing and gripped on to the handrails in front of the seat. She counted more than ten people, including one child of about twelve. *Such courage.*

"Relax," said an elderly gentleman whose eyes were as blue as the water.

She forced a smile then turned to Stephen as the boat started to move. "Did you know the river got its name from the first European that settled on Lake Wakatipu in 1860? The man named it after his business partner. George Gammie's English estate called Shotover Park. The river…"

Stephen put up a hand and gave her a reassuring smile. "Let's sit back and enjoy it. Like I said, it's safe, and you're in expert hands."

The sounds of the boat's motor over clear blue water roared in between cliff faces on either side. People screamed or laughed as she held her breath, her body shifting left to right. Stephen threw his head back and chuckled. Hair flying in the wind, the boat manoeuvred around rocks and rippling waves. Splashes of water whipped around her.

A young woman in front, with black, wavy hair and sunglasses, turned to her. "I've done this before, and it is amazing. You'll have a blast."

Gina nodded. "Good to hear."

Low brush and green trees up ahead gave her relief as she spotted brilliant colours of green. Sunlight made her squint as the boat tilted side to side, causing her stomach to want to leap out.

"This is amazing, Gina. Enjoy the scenery."

She took a calming breath and remembered the numerous times the driver had done this. It was safe, so she decided to shift her focus and let go as the driver expertly navigated over the white-water rapids and squeezed through the narrow canyon walls of the Shotover. They passed cliffs and rocky outcrops with the driver's tricky manoeuvres, twists, and turns.

A greater expanse of water, and mountains up ahead with scattered trees allowed her to lower her shoulders and savour the scenery. There was a foreshore to the side with its rocky mountains of green and beige, and an array of rocks either side evoked beauty. She took in the shadows reflected on the water and trees leaned into the rapids as people laughed. One man had lifted his hands up in the air briefly. She had to admit...it was fun.

By the end of the ride, Gina smiled at Stephen when he touched her on her arm. She leaned into the warmth of his hand.

Gina stepped out onto dry land as she grinned at others who had given her a thumbs up. She felt a thrill course through her body as they made their way to the shuttle bus back to Queenstown.

The silence on the bus as she gazed out the window made her think about how Stephen had been there for her and made her feel secure. She had seen a more responsible side to him and wondered if she'd misjudged him. Sure, he could be immature, but he had stepped up and taken responsibility for her, to reassure her, and allow her to let go.

Even when Stephen wasn't by her side, she found herself drifting into a daydream with him constantly on her mind. Dreaming about him made her wake up, sweating and aroused. If she was that excited in only a dream, what would the real thing be like?

Could she take a small risk with her heart and have a little harmless fun?

CHAPTER 20

"That boat ride was such a rush," said Stephen as they headed inside his hotel room later that night. The scent of Gina's perfume smelled like roses and cinnamon combined.

Gina followed him to the couch and sat beside him. "The jet boat. Sure."

He rested back against the couch and lifted his arms as he stared at her low cleavage. The black skintight dress with a slit on its side revealed a toned and taut physique that did so much to his own body.

"About the boat ride... I am proud of you, lady. You pushed through your fears and enjoyed the trip."

She chuckled. "I must admit, I thought I was going to die, but you reassured me. I reasoned with myself. The others on the boat were having fun, and it was contagious."

"It was." He wanted to lean in, brush those red lips and track her body from head to toe. "It's great to see you let go for once."

She angled her head. "What does that mean? I let go."

He beamed. "Sure you do—when you're asleep. But other times you're wound up tight and need to have more fun. Not everything in life is negative."

She shrugged. "I didn't say it was, but there are more bad things than good ones. We have to be on our guard, and I can't help the way I am." She pursed her lips, fire in her eyes. "I don't need you to change me. I am who I am."

He put up a hand. "I would never want that, Gina. All I am saying is that a bit of fun occasionally is healthy and can make you more productive in everything."

She rose. "I think I'll go back to my room. I don't appreciate your judgement. It's not like you can win the most responsible man of the year award."

He fought against his tight chest. "Now, wait a minute. I have businesses to my name and...never mind."

"I don't care about that. It's other times, when you're not working. You take a laissez-faire attitude to everything and that's not productive."

He got up, standing inches from her face. "Don't try to change me. I am responsible when I need to be and relaxed at other times. You should try balance some time."

She scoffed and took a step back. "Typical response. But we're judging each other."

Stephen shook his head and stepped forward, yearning to kiss that mouth, excited by the fury in her eyes. She looked sexy. "Maybe we should stop thinking and..."

Gina stood with her hands on her hips. "And what?"

He took the plunge, leaned in and kissed her, but Gina shifted and slapped him across the face. "I'm sorry. I don't know what came over me. It was irresponsible of me to kiss you when you're obviously upset." He focussed on her sad eyes, hating himself for upsetting her. "I know you let go on that boat ride, and there is so much more to you, Gina. Multiple layers, so I shouldn't judge when we're still getting to know each other."

She stared into her hands and dug her nails into her palms. A flash of red across her neck might've shown shame. "I'd better go," she said without much conviction.

"Wait. Let's not go to sleep being angry like this. Tomorrow we're heading back, and I don't want to fight like this. As I said, we need to accept each other as we are, especially as we're always growing and changing in life." She remained silent, swallowing repeatedly. Was she nervous?

She took a breath, softening. "You're right."

"How about a dance? Let's end the night with good vibes."

Gina hesitated. "Fine. But I'm only doing this to show you I can relax."

He retrieved his phone from the coffee table, clicked on his playlist and found a ballad by Marc Anthony called *My Baby You*. He pushed the play button and waved her over to him. She fell into his arms.

Stephen stroked the small of her back and held her tight against him, the feel of her hand on his shoulder arousing. He brushed the skin on her neck as he drew her closer while she wrapped both arms around his waist. He wanted her closer, without clothes between them. He needed her like he'd never needed anyone before.

His hand brushed the back of her head as she fell deeper into the crook of his shoulder, inching her waist closer against his own until he touched the middle of her back, sending tingles down his spine. When the music ended, the next song played but he stopped listening when they pulled apart, their eyes locked, heat in his loins as she parted her lips as if inviting him. He gently pressed his lips against hers, their tongues tangling in a heady mix of lust and heat.

He pulled away from her and she pulled him towards the bedroom. "Are you sure about this?" he asked.

She nodded.

With his hands over her hips, he trailed his lips over the centre of her chest. Reaching for the zipper behind her, he unzipped and it gently slipped off her. He grazed her neck, and her breasts pressed hard against his chest, the intensity of the heat causing him to moan.

As they lay on the bed, Gina slid her hands over his shirt and removed it, then rubbed his chest before planting soft kisses down to his navel. He pulled off his pants, wriggled and writhed as if he couldn't get enough of her, especially when her hand glided around the outline of his waist and upper thighs. This woman was undoing him, and he needed all of her.

"Oh, God. You make me crazy," he said as he caressed her breasts then dipped his head and licked a nipple while she pressed her body harder against him. His fingers found her bottom and he ran them over her skin, removing her underwear. She pulled them down her legs and threw them to the floor. "Let me touch you."

With her bare bottom and exposed inner thighs, he pushed and probed inside her as she hungrily devoured him with her mouth, their tongues delving deeper, licking and tenderly biting lips with an urgency he had never known before.

Gina's hands found his penis and she pleasured him with her eyes closed until he began to work her vulva with his hand, rubbing and inserting two fingers inside her while his lips sucked and nipped her breasts. Her hand pressed gently against his head as she moaned in desire, her breathing accelerated and her body inched closer against his hand. He moved to her lips and found her mouth again. Kissing heavily, he felt her hand back on his manhood as she slid her fingers from top to bottom until he pulled it away. He wanted to come inside her.

Gina closed her eyes and sucked on his lower lip until she climaxed. He felt the wetness pooling into his hand and couldn't imagine anything hotter or sexier.

Stephen retrieved a condom from his pants pocket and she smiled as if relieved. She shifted until she was sitting on top of him, then guided his penis inside her while he threaded a hand through her glossy hair and caressed the small of her back. He thrust forward and slowly inched inside her deeper and deeper, relishing how hot and hard he was getting. When he buried himself to the hilt, he saw the heated arousal in her eyes and watched her slowly lick her lips. They both shattered with their orgasms as they locked lips again, unable to get enough of each other.

CHAPTER 21

G ina roused from sleep the next morning but when she opened her eyes, she gasped. *Oh, no!* Last night. They had made love twice. Her body ached yet tingled at the same time. It was a delicious pain she wanted more of, but knew it was a one-night fantasy.

She had forgotten about Steven, forgotten about her sister, and had forgotten that men were the scum of the Earth. Stephen, in bed beside her, was not the man who wouldn't break her heart. He could not be the one who would commit to only one woman when he'd had a string of them. No, this was a one-time thing, especially considering she'd had oo much to drink. The excitement and beauty of New Zealand had taken them away from real life. This was a fantasy. Nothing more.

But how her stomach flipped at the way his full lips parted and the way his taut, muscled arms lay flat above his shoulders, leaning against the bed with the sheet draped over a tanned leg. He shifted, and the sheet fell away to reveal his erect manhood. *Holy hell!* Was he having a wet dream? Was it about her, or one of his other women?

When he slowly opened his eyes, they lit up at the sight of her watching him. "Hi there, gorgeous." It instilled more arousal, rendering her speechless. "How long have you been watching me in all my nakedness?"

She breathed in his sweaty, woody scents, wanting to devour those lips. He was like a drug. Once she got a taste of him, she needed more. "Only a few minutes."

"I see." His eyes trailed her from head to toe while the sheet lay tightly above her breasts to hide her nudity. "I am again curious as to what's underneath that sheet, and why you're gripping it for dear life. Let it go."

"Why?" Heat warmed her face, and she could barely breathe. Barely form a sentence. What was wrong with her?

"We have a few hours before our flight, so we've got time for you to scream my name and for me to make you come more than once."

"Really?" she said with a smirk across her face. "Vain much?"

He laughed. "Come over here, beautiful."

Gina leaned into his side until he flipped her onto his stomach and devoured her with his lips, his tongue gliding over her teeth and inside her mouth as if he couldn't get enough of her. His hands squeezed her buttocks as she wriggled and writhed against his penis. Oh, this man was undoing her. She didn't want to orgasm yet so she controlled herself when he shifted his hand to her inner thighs, prodding and pushing while pulling away from her mouth. "Come for me, Gina, and look at me as you do."

"Ridiculous. What about you?"

"Oh, your excitement will arouse me too, don't worry. But buck into my hand and savour the touch. I...need to see you." He pushed deeper inside her as she closed her eyes and moaned, licking her bottom lip. Opening her eyes, she spotted something unexpected in his gaze: a need, a desire she couldn't put a name to. But she let it go as the force of his hand against her mound made her further open herself up, pushing her body harder into his fingers until she became wet and climaxed. His grin could have lit up the whole room when she gazed into his eyes. Then they changed positions, with him on top of her.

Stephen wasted no time in hungrily kissing her while tugging on her upper lip and licking the back of her ear. "Oh, God. So beautiful." He leaned into her breast and sucked tenderly until moving on to the next one as she leaned hard into him to relish the warm sensation. He extended his hand to reach for a condom on the bedside table, rolled it on to his length then guided himself into her. They moved in a strong rhythm, gazing into each other's eyes with need and yearning. Stephen came before her but when she orgasmed again, the glow in his eyes made her feel alive and free. What was this man doing to her?

Gina unlocked the door with Stephen behind her, wheeling her suitcase as she set down her bags inside her living room. "Would you like a coffee?"

"No, I should get going. I've got an early meeting in the morning, and I have to prepare for it. But I had a nice time. Did you?"

She hid her disappointment, knowing they had to face reality. "New Zealand is beautiful. I'd visit again." Would he ask her out? Did she want him to?

"We might need to go again. For work, I mean. Amazing how I got the call from Jared once we were in the air. But once the centre's up and running there might be a few glitches. At least there's virtual tracking." Their eyes locked, but she looked away and played with the collar of her blouse. Her throat became parched.

"At least have a glass of water before you go. You need to stay hydrated." She didn't want him to leave just yet.

"Fine. One glass then I should head out."

She walked to the kitchen and reached for a glass, but when she looked over her shoulder Stephen was eyeing her again from head to toe. It was sexy the way he looked at her as if he yearned for her again. But was it merely wishful thinking?

He grabbed the glass and drank it down in one gulp. Was he going to leave so soon? Rather than put the glass into the sink, he held on to it. "So...ahm...you have a good rest of the night, and I'll see you at work in a few days. I'll need your business projections and data for the Mount Macedon centre, so we can take it to the board. Will you have it ready?"

Her chest tightened. "Of course. It's an amazing place and I think it will do well. Is there anything else you need?"

"Nothing. I'll be seeing you." He headed for the door, shutting it behind him after he left.

What the hell? Her breathing shallowed and her shoulders drooped. No kiss. No touch. He left as if she meant nothing to him.

Gina brushed aside the ache in her chest and wheeled her suitcase to her bedroom. What did she expect? A man like that would have his fun then move on to the next woman. She was only another notch on his belt.

But when she heard the door open, she jolted and turned around. Stephen stormed inside, took the suitcase out of her hand and smashed his lips against hers. Once he pulled away, he said, "I forgot to do this, and I hope we can keep having fun." Giving her a wink, he rushed back out the door and left her speechless.

Gina's head spun and her legs felt unsteady, so she sat on the couch and rested her head against it. This heightened sense of fantasy gave her hope that he did care for her. Was she more than a one-night stand? Did he want to keep seeing her, and could she take the risk? Touching her lips, she could still feel the buzz of his over hers.

Moments passed when a knock on the door jerked her out of her reverie. She rose and swung open the door. "Dalia. What a surprise."

"I thought I'd check in and talk to you about New Zealand with hottie. How was it?"

She rested back on the couch with Dalia beside her. "Where do I begin, Dalia? The place is beautiful, and..."

Dalia's eyes dilated as she put a hand over her mouth. "Wow. You slept with Stephen, didn't you? Don't deny it. I can see it in your eyes. Spill, woman."

Gina chuckled. "Yes, I am on such a high right now; it was out of this world. Like nothing I've ever experienced, Dalia. He was gentle and warm and knew what I liked."

"Ooh, I would be so jealous if I didn't have Luca. Tell me more."

She shrugged. "I'm kidding myself. I don't know if he'll want to see me again socially. He hasn't said anything apart from wanting to keep having fun. Is that all he sees me as: fun? I hope I'm not like one of his other women, who cling to him until he lets them go."

Dalia shook her head. "Oh, come on, Gina. Do not compare yourself with that woman at the nightclub. You have an actual friendship with him, so that's a good foundation. Give it time and see where it goes. It's early days."

"But he's way out of my league, and I can already see him breaking my heart. He'll soon get bored and move on to the next conquest. I know men like that. I don't know if I should keep having fun with him."

Dalia sighed. "Now, you're overthinking it. Enjoy the moments you have with him and let yourself feel it. Don't overthink it. Relationships take time to develop, but nothing good can happen if you keep ruminating and being negative. He might not have met the right woman, so he played the field. Nothing wrong with that. Rose did it."

"I don't know. You might be right, but I'll tread carefully and try not to get attached. But when I see him, he does things to me. The way he laughs, the way he desires me, the way he licks my upper lip, the way he makes me feel safe...especially when flying in a small plane and taking a scary boat ride. He's brilliant."

Dalia touched her shoulder. "Oh my god!" She angled her head. "You're in love with the guy, aren't you?"

She swallowed, hesitating. *No.* "Of course I'm not. I hardly know the man. It's only been a few months since we met. You're wrong. So wrong."

"Okay. If you say so," she said unconvincingly.

But Gina looked away and wondered. Could she be in love with the man? *Of course not.* It was only the change of scenery and his exciting nature that did amazing things to her.

CHAPTER 22

"**I** need a private chef to come over tonight. Please make sure it happens." He ended the call and rubbed his hands, hoping he'd come in time. He leaned back in his ergonomic chair as he scrolled through emails on his desktop computer.

It had been a week since he and Gina had slept together, and this past week had been a challenge to keep his hands off her. The way her eyes looked past him when she was nervous, or the way she tilted her head in confusion. Even the way her smooth lips felt against his, not to mention how she'd recite facts to hide her embarrassment. It was cute and sexy, and he wanted more of her.

After getting back from New Zealand, she had appeared standoffish, as if she'd regretted their intimacy, so he'd left without kissing her. But then he wondered if she only felt awkward because she was the type of woman who struggled to show emotions. He risked it and had gone back to kiss those tasty lips, and he knew he'd made the right decision. She was open to exploring something between them, and a little harmless fun couldn't hurt, so he'd invited her over to his house for dinner.

Stephen rushed into his bedroom to change his clothes when his phone buzzed. Sitting on his bed, he answered the call. "Hey, Dale. What's up?"

"What's going on with you, man? I went to your office after our meeting to discuss the new agenda items and you disappeared on me. Where did you go?"

"Sorry, Dale. I realised I wouldn't make it in time to get the private chef inside my home and I needed to be here."

"You haven't had a private chef since Katie."

He swallowed, realising he'd said too much. His feelings for Gina didn't need to be broadcasted as he wasn't sure where it was going. "It's a kind gesture."

Dale chuckled. "Are you inviting Gina over? Is that it? You didn't tell me much about your trip. What happened?"

He huffed. "Listen, I would rather not say. We are getting to know each other, but I'd like to wine and dine her."

"Sounds serious."

He shook his head as if Dale could see him. Why did that word give him an uneasy feeling? Them having sex didn't have to mean more than two friends enjoying each other. "I have to go, Dale. But we'll talk about those issues next week. Put your questions in an email so I can prepare for Monday."

"Will do."

He ended the call, threw his phone on the bed and slipped off his shirt and tie. His hands trembled as he threw on a casual, light knit jumper over loose black jeans. His heart raced and his palms dampened when the doorbell rang. Swallowing, he rushed to the door with his eyes lighting up at the sight of Gina, who wore a low-cut red blouse over a long black skirt. In his mind, she was wearing too much clothing and yearned to undress her right on his doorstep.

"Hi, Gina." He leaned in and kissed her tenderly on the lips. She reciprocated, and then he guided her inside. "Welcome to my humble abode." Her eyes darted in all directions. Was she impressed? Not that he needed to impress her, but his chest lifted at the idea she felt comfortable in his home.

As he was about to close the door behind her, a tall man wearing a chef's hat scurried inside with a wave. "So sorry I am late. Granddaughter trouble, Mr Farrugiya."

"Not a problem. The maid is through there and she will get you prepared."

He nodded, though the poor man looked flushed. "Of course, sir. Thank you. I will be a little over an hour."

"All good, Sergio.".

Gina frowned. "You have a chef?"

Stephen shrugged as he led her to his sofa. "Not daily but intermittently when I..."

"You want to impress a girl?"

"Sure." He wrapped his arms around her and stroked the small of her back as he backed her into the couch. "Not just any girl. A beautiful and captivating woman." He flicked a strand of hair out of her eye, loving the scent of roses and soap as he planted his lips on hers, their tongues dancing as he pressed his body hard against hers, moaning. "Oh, you make me crazy, Gina. So crazy."

She pulled away and fixed the top of her blouse, which had fallen down her shoulder. "We need to be aware there are other people in this amazing house. Don't forget that."

Stephen would enjoy seeing his staff members catch them while making love, but he wouldn't do that to them. Yet the adrenaline thrill of making love to her in each of his rooms made his manhood harden. What was wrong with him? He'd never felt this strongly about showing off his woman. But was she his woman or were they only having fun?

Gina walked beside Stephen on her grand tour of the mansion, stepping inside the spacious kitchen with its marble countertops, matte floorboards, stainless steel fridge with a push-button ice machine and coffeemaker, tall decorative lamps, and a solid oak table that was almost as long as her apartment. Round mirrors opposite the table and in the lounge area gave the illusion of space, and abstract paintings and portraits hung on the walls. "I love the space here." The chef cracked eggs then beat them with a whisk as he smiled in their direction. She couldn't believe he'd paid for a private chef, but he liked to impress. No doubt he'd done this with other women. She wasn't special.

But Christ, the way he kissed was like she'd never been kissed before, and the way he touched her in all the right places, made her want to scream his name. She couldn't be falling for the man when he'd hurt her in the end, but why not let herself go occasionally? They were both adults, and this didn't need to mean anything, despite him being on her mind all day every day.

"Let me show you the bedrooms." After stepping inside all four bedrooms, he showed her his. A large TV was suspended over a glossy white timber cabinet and a matching desk stood opposite. The desk was scattered with bulging in-trays, two open laptops, and a few pens haphazardly arranged underneath papers and around a desktop computer. A landscape painting hung over his bed, which featured a leather headboard and silky beige quilt. On either side were white timber venetian blinds partially drawn, creating a cosy ambience.

Stephen squeezed her shoulder after closing the bedroom door. "Why not a predinner delight?"

Gina's heart palpitated. "What? No, not now. It wouldn't be proper with your staff here. What would they think?"

"My maid knows to not disturb me when my door's closed but she'll be leaving soon, and the chef will be busy in the kitchen for the next forty-five minutes or so. Come here."

Gina looked over her shoulder as if someone might come in at any moment. This man was making her stretch her boundaries, and a part of her relished it. What harm could there be in enjoying each other while they waited?

She took off her wedged heels and lay them neatly on the carpet. Then fell into his arms and lay on top of him when he squeezed her bottom and delved hungrily into her mouth. She couldn't get enough of the minty taste of his mouth. Her underwear became damp when he flipped her over, lifted her skirt, and lay on his stomach while lowering himself down the bed. What was he doing?

"I hope you don't mind." She was lost for words and shook her head, the need for him to excite her surpassing all reasoning. She didn't want to think but would enjoy his mouth over her body.

Stephen slowly pulled down her underwear, licking his lips as he threw them to the side. He spread her legs wide and the air between her thighs made her wetter. But when his lips trailed the side of her thighs, she bucked against him and closed her eyes to savour his sweet kisses. "You are beautiful." His mouth reached closer to her opening when he probed a finger inside her before inserting another. "I want you to enjoy me tasting you, Gina." When his body lifted to get closer to her mound, she came undone with arousal. He pressed his lips against her private parts and flicked his tongue inside. He moaned before staring up at her with a wide grin. She wriggled and writhed while pulling his head deeper inside her, his mouth licking and sucking with vigour. He held tight onto her legs as he spread her even wider. She couldn't breathe and loved the way his mouth felt against her. This was madness. What if those outside heard her desires and muffled words?

Her legs spread wide with her skirt gathered around her, she gyrated when she orgasmed and screamed his name. "Oh, Stephen. Yes, yes!" His lips trailed her legs after she came.

He lifted himself up and reached her mouth, then kissed her hard until removing his jeans and underwear. "Oh, Gina. Wow. Sexy." He stroked her cheek before making mad, passionate love to her. Why did he make her mind turn to mush?

CHAPTER 23

Gina had still been flushed after their erotic encounter when the chef had called them for dinner. Luckily, they weren't in the middle of sex at the time. Now seated in the living room, the dish the man set in front of her smelled rich, of herbs, pepper, and pork.

The chef had an easy smile as he explained the dish. "This is a Japanese Pork Fried Rice Omelette with Okonomiyaki Sauce. I learned this while working in Japan. It is a dish called Omurice, a traditional Japanese egg dish, whipped up by adding fried rice with an omelette. The dish is made with pork and drizzled with sweet-savoury okonomiyaki sauce."

Gina picked up her fork. "It smells amazing. Thank you."

"Yes, thank you, Sergio. We will delve right in."

He nodded. "I will be back with the second dish when you are ready." He made his way back to the kitchen.

She took a few bites and appreciated the sweetness and tang of the sauce. "Who would have thought you could make fried rice with an omelette in this shape? It's tasty."

Stephen devoured his food. "Yes, it's one of his best dishes."

Gina was curious. "How often do you use his services?" His eyes peered past her as if he was remembering something. "Stephen?"

He shrugged. "Not often, but possibly every few months."

"When was the last time he cooked for you?"

Stephen hesitated. "I was with Katie." He averted his eyes. "She loved trying new dishes and I wanted to surprise her before she..." The ache in Gina's heart made her wince.

She held back tears. "I am sorry. I didn't mean to upset you."

Again, he hesitated, but then squared his shoulders. "It's okay. She wanted to travel to Japan but we never got the chance."

Gina frowned. "That's tough, Stephen. Did you ever talk to someone about your grief?"

He shook his head. "What would that have accomplished? I had to move on." His eyes misted. "Let's talk about something else."

Gina reached for his hand and gave him a reassuring smile. "Of course."

The chef interrupted their moment. "Are you ready for the next dish?" Stephen nodded, and the chef returned with a soup dish. "Here we have a Japanese seafood soup. It consists of squid, ginger, and tuna." He set the dishes on the table. "Enjoy."

Gina slurped her soup, tasting the spices and seafood. It was heavenly. "Delicious."

"I have a confession to make about your artwork."

She tilted her head. "Oh?"

He leaned forward. "I spoke to an artist friend of mine who's agreed to take on your paintings in the next few months for his upcoming gallery showing. I showed him the work you sent me on your phone, and he loves it."

The taste of the soup fell into the back of her mind as her shoulders sank. What had he done? This wasn't how she wanted to get into a gallery showing. With favours. She needed to do this for herself. It felt like her father was controlling her all over again. Never accepting her as only Gina but as to what she could achieve "Are you serious?"

His eyes looked blank. "Of course. You have talent. It shouldn't be wasted. You'll have a few months to create more pieces and it'll be a full house."

Gina scoffed. "I never asked you to do that. Why would you?" She regretted him gently encouraging her to send some of her paintings, knowing the right thing to say.

Stephen's eyes darkened as he fidgeted with his hands and put aside his spoon. The chef was busy preparing the next dish. "I'm sorry, Gina. I was only trying to help. What's the big deal? I know you didn't want your paintings to catch dust in your home. I was doing you a favour."

"A favour? I don't need your favours. I was planning to get my work out there in my own time and I don't need you controlling my life. My passion. How dare you do that without my consent? I never thought..."

He squinted. "Never thought what?"

"Nothing."

"I did what I thought you'd appreciate."

"I want you to cancel it as I'm not interested."

"But why? You're talented." She remained tight-lipped. "I'm sorry, but can't you accept that I only wanted to help? Let things go as they should sometimes."

Gina turned to the chef, who stood by awkwardly until Stephen ushered him over.

"Okay," Serge said. "The next dish we have is Japanese chicken wings with a dash of garlic, hoisin sauce, honey, and a soy and vinegar sauce. I'll be back with the dessert soon."

"Don't bother," said Gina. "If you haven't made it, I'm fine to finish with this dish. Thank you, Sergio."

He nodded. "As you wish, Gina."

"Please," said Stephen. "Let's talk about this."

She sighed. "Let's eat our dish and not speak. I don't want to talk in circles."

Gina barely tasted the dish as she sat back in her chair, avoided his eyes, and dug into her chicken wings. When she was done, she got up from her chair, headed over to the coffee table where her bag lay, and turned to him. "Goodbye, Stephen."

He inched his way forward. "Wait. That sounds final."

"I think this was a mistake. You're my client, so maybe we shouldn't have mixed business with pleasure."

"Are you breaking this off?" His eyes appeared to be pools of darkness.

"I don't know. I need space to think. Please give me that." He nodded, his body stiffening.

She swung the door open with a heavy heart, then closed it behind her without gazing back and ran to her car. Once inside, she bowed over her steering wheel and fought back tears, and then started the motor and sped off. She didn't dare look back at the house, for fear he was watching from the window. Had she made the right decision? *Of course*. But why did her heart clench as if she was about to pass out?

CHAPTER 24

Stephen leaned back in his chair two days after having dinner with Gina, rubbing his palms as she spoke at the head of the conference table. A projector opposite displayed a spreadsheet and graphs.

He couldn't hate himself more for hurting her when it hadn't been his intention. It was done out of...well, who knew what he was starting to feel for Gina, but he wasn't ready to let her go. Not when they'd only just started.

His heart raced at the way she brushed the middle of her neck, flaming red in the cheeks as she calmly took a breath. The simple black skirt matched with a white blouse and jacket made her look sexy. He wanted to caress those cheeks and brush over her quivering lip as she clasped papers in her hands and whispered to Teresa.

Nine of his staff members gazed in Gina's direction, leaning forward with pens in hand.

Jeanie touched him on the shoulder, lingering. "Are you all right?" She had an easy smile and looked younger than her thirty years.

"I'm fine. Just focussing." The hungry look she gave him unnerved him.

Dianne sat on his other side. "Is something going on between you and Gina?" she whispered.

"Let's listen to the presentation, shall we?"

"Of course. Sorry," said Dianne.

When he faced Gina, she bit her bottom lip, squared her shoulders and clasped her hands together. Was she jealous? Jeanie had touched him, but did Gina believe it was more than friendly? Not that she knew their casual sexual history.

Gina stood alongside the projector screen and pushed the remote button. "This here is a baseline figure versus the figures over the past quarter. As you can see, we've had a noticeable increase in rates of enquiry that have led to strong conversions. Managing three different health centres' locations, our campaign data, which displayed customer preferences and trends, allowed us to better tailor our services to meet market demand. We know what the customer wants in these three areas." She pointed to the screen. "Teresa improved the landing page experience, SEO, and arranged Google search advertising. What we've seen so far," she pointed to the graph on the screen, "is a six per cent conversion rate, so we project that within a financial year it will increase to at least twenty-four per cent."

Rob asked, "What about the data on the Geelong health hub? How did that help?"

Stephen switched off as he'd seen the data before the meeting and so desperately wanted to talk to her. He was itching to repair the rift between them. Gina was a master in her work, and he couldn't imagine not having her in his life.

At the end of the meeting, his team slowly left the room. Teresa waved a hand. "I will see you in a few days, Stephen, for the fund-raising party in the city."

"Of course, and thank you for your hard work. See you Saturday." With a brief smile, she walked out and left him alone with Gina. She opened up her satchel and inserted documents while acting as if he wasn't there. *Say something*. "Gina, I am so sorry for going behind your back. I will talk to my friend and explain you're not ready or that you have another interested buyer."

She packed up her laptop and pushed it inside her satchel. "It's fine. But I don't appreciate you going behind my back. I need to do... I have to...have to know that I can achieve things on my own. I do not need hand-outs."

He nodded. "I get that. You're a strong, independent woman and I won't get in the way of you doing this at your pace. You have so much talent." He spread out his arms. "In this and your artwork."

She closed her satchel. "Don't think I can forgive you that easily. I am still mad, and need you to know that I don't like underhanded actions. It burned me with my ex and my sister; I need to feel respected."

"It was never my intention to disrespect you in any way, shape, or form, Gina. I only did it because..." How could he tell her he cared more than he wanted to admit? "I did it because you have talent and my artist friend needs artists, but in your own time."

Gina's eyes turned dark for a fleeting moment. "Fine then."

He edged closer and squeezed her shoulder. Her eyes softened as he gently traced the outline of her lips with his hand and she leaned into it, moaning. "Hold that thought." He rushed over to the door and locked it. He leaned in and kissed her hungrily, but she pulled back when he tilted his head, curious.

"Wait," she said. "What's with Jeanie? She hates me."

He didn't want to upset her again, so he decided not to mention their fling from one year ago. "She might be threatened by you. You're accomplished."

Her eyes fixed on him as if she wasn't convinced. "Okay. I'd better go."

Stephen nodded. "See you soon for the work party."

Gina smiled before opening the door and rushing out. Why did he feel like a jerk for not telling her about Jeanie? But it wasn't the right time.

CHAPTER 25

Saturday arrived and Gina's heart raced as she stepped out of the limousine Stephen had hired for her, Teresa, Rob, Dianne, Jeanie, and Dale. The building for the fund-raising party appeared old with a red-brick façade.

Her spine tingled when Stephen touched the small of her back and led her through a narrow walkway into a dimly lit space with a mixture of modern facilities and old-world décor.

Stephen leaned in towards two towering blonde women who wore Venetian masks. "Hey, Laurie, Jo. Is everything ready?"

"As you requested, Mr Farrugiya. Come inside," said Laurie who waved them in while his team and Teresa walked in behind her.

"What's going on?" asked Gina.

He gave her a cheeky grin. "You'll see."

They stepped into a vast room, her heels digging into plush green carpet with swirly patterns and a green couch a mile long, which featured chequered designs. Upside down cones used as tables stood opposite padded settees.

Teresa linked arms with her. "Wow. This is beautiful. So spacious." She pointed to a giant portrait of a face with hair made of assorted vegetables.

Gina laughed. "You are what you eat." Teresa nodded while Stephen greeted men in suits who wore Venetian masks. Women wore cocktail attire with masks too. Was this a masquerade party?

Stepping through a bar with a dance area and lights shining on the glossy floor, a woman juggling sticks of fire beamed in Stephen's direction. Heat emanated and sweat rose on the back of Gina's neck.

A bartender shook a container and filled a martini glass with some concoction. Smells of coffee, beer, spices, and colognes filled her senses as people scattered across different areas of the room, all holding drinks. Servers bustled about, offering trays of finger foods. At least thirty people had arrived before them.

Gina walked beside Stephen, who turned to her and the team and directed their attention to a wall featuring a range of masks. "Guys, I'd like you to pick any mask you like. We are going to enjoy this masquerade party with an air of mystery, and a game to come later in the night."

Gina frowned. "You've gone all out, Stephen. How much did this cost you? The event planning, the masks, food, and snacks. Even the fire juggling bartender."

He kissed her briefly on the lips. "Anything for my team, and you, of course." With a stroke of her cheek, he faced the team who stared with wide eyes. Her heart raced. Were they in an official relationship?

"Ooh, I love this one," said Teresa, picking one that looked like eyeglasses.

Gina leaned in and watched the others pull masks from the wall before she found one she loved. Unpinning it from the wall, she gazed at the black lace mask with its floral design and pearls over a thin fabric. A black flower was attached to the side. She put it on.

Stephen brushed her bottom lip. "I love that on you. Beautiful."

She swallowed, aware of how his body brushed against hers. She couldn't get enough of this man. "What about yours?"

He nodded and selected one. "This one. It's Roman, made of strong plastic and I love the details in this design."

Gina stared at the man from head to toe, admiring his black suit over a fitted white shirt and tie. He looked very much like the billionaire he was, and she yearned to hold him in her arms. Scents of musk and his hand caressing the inside of her palm made her heart flutter. What was wrong with her? She couldn't be falling for him, could she?

Once his team had put on their masks, he led them towards another room while he greeted more guests with waves and nods. The space was inviting with its black vinyl padded booths and rounded seating, with more upside down cones as tables. They sat around the area where, behind them, golden-coloured windows showcased a quaint garden setting. Beside the bar was a painting of a woman's face. An opaque glass ceiling suited the dark ambience of the room. People stood at the edge of the dance floor, a few dancing to the strong rhythms of a raunchy jazz song, underneath a disco light. A new set of servers ambled about with trays of canapes.

Stephen put up a hand when a petite male waiter approached. "We're ready for a few trays of the finger foods that I selected, and champagne all around." He looked at his team, who sat opposite her, with him and Teresa on either side.

"You've outdone yourself," said Dianne, whose red mini dress made her look like a top model.

"I so agree," said Jeanie, whose dark eyes scrutinised her. Was she not happy about Gina and Stephen?

Rob patted Stephen on the shoulder. "You should be getting your money's worth for heart research."

"That is the plan," said Stephen.

His friend, Dale, scanned the women. "You all look lovely tonight ladies, and those masks give you an air of mystery. I would probably not recognise some of you."

Gina laughed. "I'm sure you could recognise me. This mask barely covers my face."

Stephen tenderly held her hand over his thigh. "I can't imagine anyone wouldn't want to see this gorgeous face."

Teresa chuckled. "My sentiments exactly."

Gina shook her head. "Oh, please. I don't need flattery."

Jeanie leaned forward. "How long have you two been together?" They were saved from having to answer immediatley when two servers arrived carrying a bucket of champagne and a tray of glasses. They poured drinks for everyone.

"Not long," said Stephen as Gina stiffened beside him.

What was Jeanie's problem? Did she have a crush on Stephen?

CHAPTER 26

Stephen's heart fluttered each time he saw Gina. The sequined black fitted dress with thin straps displayed all her feminine curves, triggering the desire to tantalise her in a private room. More of that later.

His reverie broke when the waiter arrived with a box of notes. *Ah, yes, the mystery game.* "Here you are, sir."

"Thank you," Stephen said. He got up and walked over to a small stage and spoke into the microphone. "Can I have your attention please?"

All eyes were on him as everyone stopped talking. "We are going to play a mystery game where you'll come up to this table." He pointed to a stack of name tags piled high on the table opposite. "The waiters will give you a name tag that reveals either a famous character like Romeo and Juliet or celebrities like Beyonce and Jay Z." He scanned the room. "It's important that you don't reveal who you are as it defeats the purpose of the mystery. The aim of the game is to find the guest whose nametag matches yours. You can only ask yes or no questions, so players need to reply with a yes or no. You are not allowed to ask directly about a character or celebrity's name, like, 'does your name start with a D?' If you think you've found your match, the waiter over there will confirm it. Then, when you're finished, you can wear your name tag. Any questions?"

Rob waved a hand. "Do you get to play too, Mr Boss?"

"Yes, but I don't know who my match is. It's a mystery for me too." He hoped he had Gina as his match, but he didn't want special treatment.

Gina huffed. "I love a challenge. How long do we have to find our match?"

He shrugged. "By midnight. Also, we'll have three winners who find their match the quickest. Let's get started."

When the team secured their nametags and then scattered, Stephen approached Gina and held her chin before kissing her hungrily. "I've wanted to do that again. Now go find your match. I already know we're not paired."

Gina smiled then made her way towards the guests, the sway of her hips arousing him. She approached a man who got far too close to her, but he remembered this was a game and she'd be moving on if he wasn't her match.

Stephen wandered around, his mind ruminating on what he planned to do to Gina later that night. He had never met anyone like her; a strong-willed woman who had a creative side through her art. She was talented and beautiful, with a good heart, but he felt a sadness inside of her. Something caused by more than her relationship with her sister. In her own time, he hoped she'd explain why.

When half an hour had passed and he still hadn't found his match, he continued to roam the room until coming face to face with Jeanie.

She leaned in and pointed back over her shoulder. "How about you and I get out of here, boss? Like old times."

"Are you drunk?"

She shook her head. "Only had a couple of glasses, Stephen. How about it?"

"That's all it takes to get you drunk. You never could take your alcohol." He stepped back but she inched forward.

"I know you like it rough. You can't tell me that Gina satisfies you the way I did. Let me show you how much I've missed you. I want to taste you all over and get you to taste me too. The way we used to, with cream and champagne over my...."

He shook his head and ushered her back to the table. "If you can't play this game, you should take a time out. Drink water." She rested against the seat when his eyes darted. His body stilled when he saw Gina frozen in place and staring at him. He had to explain.

Rushing in her direction, she turned away, but he grabbed her gently by the arm. "Wait. She's drunk, so I had to help her."

She stepped back. "It's fine. But was there ever something between you two?"

He hesitated, wanting to be truthful. "We went out a couple of times but nothing serious. She wanted more but I didn't feel the same way."

Her eyes darkened. "You could've told me that earlier. I understand now why she hates me. I'd better get mingling." It didn't sound good when her voice shook like that. Did she not trust him?

After finding his match, Cleopatra, later that night, and confirming it with the server, he walked outside and headed to a landscaped garden that featured a water fountain, a bed of roses, and cluster of trees. He sat on a bench and savoured the warm evening breeze as he thought about Gina. What would happen when they no longer worked together? Would they part ways? A part of him wasn't sure about where they were going, but for now, why overthink it?

Muffled tears behind him made him turn. Was someone crying? Over his shoulder, he spotted Gina hunched beside a tree, dabbing at her eyes as her whole body shivered.

He walked over and put a hand on her shoulder. "Gina. What's wrong?"

She wiped away her tears. "I'm fine. I didn't know you were here. Sorry. I'm going to go." Her body shook, and she was unsteady on her feet. He pulled her back and wrapped his arms around her. "I'm okay."

He stroked her spine. "No, you are not okay. What happened? Did someone upset you? Please tell me."

She pulled away as he inched closer to her. "I... It's all good. I get sensitive sometimes, that's all. It's nothing. Let's forget it."

He looked her squarely in the eyes, his heart breaking at seeing her in pain. Was this part of the sadness he felt she hid? "We are in a relationship now, Gina, and I... I want you to be honest with me. Share your pain and I'll understand. Truly." He waited.

She sighed and rubbed the inside of her palm. "I spoke to my match. We were Nicole Kidman and Keith Urban." She wiped her tears with a tissue. He frowned, not seeing the problem. "Nicole Kidman miscarried, and it reminded me of..."

His chest ached. "Gina. Did you lose a baby?" He watched her tremble again and she slowly nodded until he pulled her into his arms. She cried her heart out. "I am so sorry." He threaded his hands through her hair. "Words cannot tell you how much."

She sniffed and remained in his arms. "Mine was most likely due to stress after hearing about my ex-boyfriend and my sister. Stillborn. I wish I'd taken better care of myself."

"No, you cannot blame yourself, Gina. These things happen and don't necessarily have a cause. I know you would have done everything right. You have a good heart."

She pursed her lips. "Thank you. I needed to hear that. But I still feel overwhelmed whenever I hear about miscarriages and stillbirths. I get triggered."

"It will always hurt, because you're human and you care about people. But so much in life we cannot control." He stroked the back of her neck, wanting to take all her pain away. "I am glad you shared that with me. It couldn't have been easy."

"I am sorry. I didn't want to burden you with this. I'm truly fine now." She gave him a reassuring smile as he smoothed a strand of hair out of her eye. *God, she was beautiful.* He could never tire of looking at her.

"You know, when I lost Katie, it was the worst pain ever, but events like tonight's give me comfort because we're raising funds for heart research. Have you thought about a ritual to help or give you comfort?"

She nodded. "I have, but it still feels raw. Perhaps one of these days I'll find something new to honour my beautiful daughter."

He felt tears sting his eyes, his chest squeezing tight. "Daughter?"

"Yes. She would have been beautiful, and I always imagine what she'd be like now at her age. Two years old. The moments we would have had, the time she would talk, walk, ride a bicycle, go to school, become a rebellious teenager..."

He chuckled and rubbed the back of her neck. "She sounds amazing, and would have been as beautiful and as smart as you." He wiped her eyes, which streamed more tears, then rubbed his own.

"Thanks, Stephen. So much."

A twig snapped behind him when one of the young male servers scurried towards him. "Sir, we have all the matches and several winners. Would you like to announce them? It's time."

"Of course. I'll be right there." He got up. "Are you okay for us to leave?"

"Yes, I'm ready."

He pulled her by the hand as they made their way back inside. If he was a betting man, he'd say he was falling in love with this brilliant woman beside him, and it scared the hell out of him.

CHAPTER 27

G ina watched the man on stage. The way he'd consoled her outside and listened to her story. She had underestimated him, thinking he was too playful and carefree while there were many layers to Stephen. Her heart soared as she realised she was falling in love with him. But how could she when she didn't know if he'd protect her heart? If she could fully trust the man?

"We have Teresa and her partner, Dale, who were the third-fastest in getting their match. Great work, guys." Loud applause filled the room as Teresa and Dale approached the stage. They picked up a hamper of goodies filled with assorted healthy snacks and beverages. They returned to Gina's side when Stephen announced the second prize.

"Congratulations, Teresa and Dale." Gina grinned at her friend.

"I'm sure you'll be up there," Teresa whispered.

"I doubt it," Gina said.

"Piece of cake," said Dale as he winked at Gina.

Stephen read the next winner. "The second prize goes to Rob and Mari. Congratulations, Rob and his partner, Mari." The pair shuffled to the stage and shook Stephen's hand. He retrieved his prize of a wellness basket while a woman Gina didn't recognise smiled and grabbed another basket.

"The winners, who were the absolute fastest to find their match are Gina and Joe." Stephen's eyes lit up as he clapped while she approached him.

"Thank you," she said as she picked up her prize: a spa and pampering package. She smiled at Joe whose eyes lit up as he reached for his similar prize. The man mentioned working as a yoga instructor in Geelong.

Stephen leaned in towards her. "Are you all right?"

She beamed. "I am surprised. But it was a great mystery game."

"Listen, Gina, I have a special surprise for us. Are you up for staying back with me? No pressure."

She had perked up since confiding her tragic story and wanted to move on. She respected that he had asked for permission; which showed he was considerate and caring. Why would she not want to spend more time with him? "I'd love to."

People waved goodbye to each other as the party fizzled out while Stephen, Teresa, and his team remained. They approached.

"Listen, guys, Gina and I will be staying back, but your limousine is waiting outside."

"Ooh," said Dianne. "What are you two up to?"

The others removed their masks and pinned them back on the wall. Jeanie glared in her direction.

"None of your business," said Stephen. He waved goodbye to Teresa and his team before pulling her away towards the drapes. "Come over here, Gina."

Her eyes widened as she gazed at a small, darkened room that featured a white, round bed with rose petals. A small couch with suspended white lights shone down on the carpet. To one side was a speaker, and beside that was a bucket of champagne. "What is this?"

"We have this room for the night. The staff are leaving, and they'll be back in the morning. I thought you deserved this treat."

She felt a spring in her step. No-one had ever put in so much effort for her before. "This is too much, Stephen. Is this because of what I said?"

He grabbed her by the waist. "No, it was planned a few days ago. Only the best for you." He retrieved his phone from his back pocket and clicked on a few buttons. A slow ballad came out of the speaker, a song she didn't recognise, but it set the romantic mood. "Dance with me."

She wrapped her arms around him as they swayed to the music. Her body was on fire and her legs felt like jelly. Even her hands sweated as he tightened his grip around her waist and she lay her head on his shoulder. Gina closed her eyes and relished the way their bodies melded like glue, how his touch drew her closer towards him. When the song ended, he pulled away and poured them each a glass of champagne.

"To us," he said as he handed her a glass.

"To us," Gina reciprocated. Taking a sip, the cold drink soothed her parched throat. Still nervous, she spilled it on her cleavage and the top of her dress. "Oh, no. I've ruined the dress."

"Let me." He put down his glass on the table and then inched forward to lick her chest clean. "You're so beautiful."

Gina got aroused as his tantalising lips trailed kisses down the centre of her chest. He gently pushed her to the bed. His hand caressed the middle of her throat as he planted gentle kisses over it. She moved back and savoured his kisses until her arousal heightened when she felt his manhood harden.

With a gentle finger, he probed in between her thighs. "Do you like this?"

She took slow breaths and closed her eyes, feeling herself getting wet. "Yes."

"How about this?" He probed two fingers inside her.

"God, yes."

Stephen slowly unzipped her and pulled her out of the dress while he stayed fully clothed. He licked his lips then pulled aside her hair to kiss the side of her neck while taking off her underwear. His heated kisses over her arms sent tingles all over as she gently held his head over her body. His mouth reached her belly but then he stopped to retrieve his glass.

"You're having a drink now?" asked Gina.

"Yes, on you." Slowly, he spilled drizzles of champagne over her belly and licked her clean as if he was dying of thirst. "My god, Gina. I cannot get enough of you." He poured more of the drink down her private parts and lapped her up, feasting on her as if she was his last meal. She couldn't describe her arousal, as it was like she was in heaven, his tongue delving deep inside and licking her dry. Once she climaxed, he lifted himself up and kissed her hungrily, tasting herself on his lips.

She spent the remainder of the night making love with this brilliant man until spooning herself against him in bed. What more could he do to surprise her? She was in heaven and didn't want whatever this was to end.

CHAPTER 28

"Keep your voice down, Dalia. People can hear you," said Gina, who sat outside a café, sipping on a latte while her friend enjoyed the remainder of her cappuccino. Why had she told Dalia what had happened two nights ago at the masquerade party?

Dalia rested back against her chair. "I'm sorry, but I can't believe how much effort he went into giving you the best night of your life. None of your ex-boyfriends were like that. I can see it in your eyes. You're in love with the guy."

Gina shook her head. "I don't know. Maybe it's the excitement of it all. He knows how to treat a woman." Her memory flashed back to the way he smoothly caressed the back of her fingertips or brushed the corner of her lip with his gentle thumb. Who wouldn't be swept off their feet by a billionaire, and a handsome one at that?

"When are you seeing him again?" Dalia asked.

"In a few days. We have to talk about marketing and prelaunch options for the new health centre he plans to open in Mount Macedon. I don't want our working relationship to suffer, but this thing we have... I can't stop thinking about him. Oh, Dalia, he is always on my mind, day and night, and I don't even have an appetite around him. What's wrong with me?"

Dalia chuckled. "It's called love, darling. Embrace it and enjoy yourself. It's not often you get to relax and have fun. All work and no play makes for a dull life."

Gina waved a hand then bit into a brioche. "I have to take it slow as I'm starting to feel overwhelmed by it all. But the other night took me to another place. We were in another dimension. He made me feel things I didn't know I could feel and..." She felt her face warm.

"The sex was hot, right? I know it's hard for you to talk about that stuff, Gina, but it's natural. Perfectly natural to enjoy making love with the man you love."

Gina ate the remainder of her sweet and stared past Dalia, whose eyes brightened. When was the last time she felt on top of the world, like she could conquer anything? Any obstacle, any conflict. "Oh, and the way he listened and comforted me when I talked about the loss of my daughter. He was there for me. Not many men would listen the way he did, or put up with my crying."

Dalia touched her hand. "Oh, Gina. You deserve to cry when you think about your little girl. I can't imagine going through such trauma."

Gina pushed back tears. "Thanks, Dalia, but I'll be okay."

"Have you thought about reconciling with your sister? Forgiveness can help you to heal. Family's important."

She shook her head. "I can't. Not right now." Gina clasped her hands together and swallowed, wondering if her parents would ever stop hounding her about talking to Toni. Her sister had tried countless times to ask for forgiveness, but Gina couldn't do it.

Stephen winced at the way Dale slapped him hard on the back. "Lighten up, will you? It was not much effort on my part."

Dale laughed as they sat inside the conference room, scrutinising spreadsheets on their laptops. "You could've fooled me. A romantic escape in that monumental mansion, the music, dark ambience, circular bed, champagne... No easy feat. You must love this woman."

Stephen brushed him off. "Why don't we figure out the budget and expenses for the new Mount Macedon centre? I think we should hire another osteopath if we want to turn a profit. It might cost us more in the short-term, but in the long run, it's more financially viable."

"I hear you, and I agree, but don't deflect. I'd like to know how you feel about Gina. What gives?"

Stephen huffed. "Okay, I care about her. But love? We're only having fun, enjoying ourselves. We haven't known each other that long, and right now we need to focus on the business at hand. What is between Gina and me is private."

"But what if she's the one, man?"

Stephen's body quivered. He leaned in towards his laptop, clicking on keys to add in the cost for an extra osteopath. "You're getting way ahead of yourself. I don't plan to marry the woman or have babies with her, so please don't put that kind of pressure on me. You know exactly what I went through with Katie, and I can't focus on more than this."

Dale got up and stretched, then sat back down. "What is *this*, exactly?"

Stephen wondered what it was, but he couldn't deny she was always on his mind throughout the day and in his dreams. The way she flushed over his impulsive actions or the way she clenched her slender hands when irate, and even the way she bit her bottom lip when nervous. He loved all her quirks, her realism, her black and white thinking, her creativity, and her mind. But was it love? He didn't know, but then again, maybe it was love. Oh, he needed to get out of here and go for a jog. "How about we call it a day?"

Dale arched a brow. "Sure, man. You must be in love if you're not working a full Sunday. It's only one o'clock. Seriously. It's a love fever. I get it."

Stephen gave him a playful shove. "I love you, my friend, but I've had enough of your company for today. I'll have to see your ugly face again tomorrow."

Dale laughed. "You love me."

Stephen closed his laptop and gathered his briefcase before placing his device inside. He made his way out of the room and down to the underground carpark, waving goodbye to Dale before stepping inside his car.

He missed Gina. What if he dropped by her place? His body stilled until he started the motor, having made the decision. He'd surprise her.

Avoiding the busy main roads, he drove around the back streets until he reached Gina's house. Parking by the curb, he spotted a blue sedan and wondered who was visiting. Was it her friend, Dalia?

Stephen shuffled his feet after he rang the doorbell and waited.

The door swung open but the look on Gina's face wasn't what he was expecting. "This is a surprise."

His chest tightened. "Do you have company?" A woman's voice rang out. "Who is it, darling?"

Gina gave him a reassuring smile. "Come inside."

Stephen's heart raced when he spotted a middle-aged man and woman sitting on the couch with hot beverages in their hands. His heart beat a mile a minute.

"This is my mother, Josephine, and my father, Felice." She waved to him. "This is...Stephen."

Josephine wore a tight bun and had kind, blue eyes and a short stature. She stood up. "It's great to finally meet you, Stephen."

She must have spoken about him to her parents. His hands sweated and his legs felt heavy. Why did he have to come today of all days?

Felice rose alongside her, and sported a short beard with dark, stern eyes, currently fixed on him. "Stephen. Pleasure."

He took deep breaths as they assessed him. The quiet was awkward until Gina broke the ice. "Would you like a drink? You must be exhausted after working today."

He nodded. "Sure, but I'll get myself water. Nothing too strong." He made a beeline to the kitchen and found a glass in an overhead cupboard. Why did he have to meet her parents now? Surely, they'd have expectations? Maybe he could excuse himself and make a quick exit.

Heading back to the living room, he sat in the armchair opposite Gina who was sitting on the couch beside her mother. Her hands fidgeted in her lap.

Felice squinted and clasped his hands together. "Gina tells me you're setting up new health centres in New Zealand and Mount Macedon. Busy boy. How do you find time to relax with a beautiful woman?" He turned to his wife. "Like my wife, of course."

He got his breath back when he realised that she might not have told her parents about their relationship. Did her parents believe they were only colleagues?

CHAPTER 29

Stephen lost his breath, his grip tightening on his glass. He sipped quickly and forced a smile. "I manage to find a balance, sir."

Gina blushed. "We are busy getting everything set up, the pre-launch, then the launch phase." She touched the base of her throat.

Felice leaned forward. "How's the possible relocation going, Gina?"

Stephen frowned and turned to Gina. "Relocation?"

She hesitated and stared at her hands. "Dalia's boyfriend, Luca, has business contacts in Queensland. He might have the perfect building for my new marketing business. It's got everything I need."

Stephen's head spun. Was she planning to leave Victoria?

Felice nodded. "Any plans for when you might start? I assume they can't hold the space for long..."

Gina shrugged. "I still have time to work it out, but I'll need to make a decision soon, Dad."

"I would expect so," said Felice.

Stephen's body sagged as he realised he needed to get out of there.

Gina kept her eyes away from him. "Tell me what's new with both of you."

Her mother said, "Oh, honey. We had dinner with Toni and her new boyfriend. It looks like they're getting serious. He's a lovely boy, and perhaps one day you could...I don't know...drop in. She's staying in Melbourne for a few weeks."

Gina's eyes darkened and her body stiffened. "Mum, please. We've talked about this. I can't. I am sorry, but please, I just can't. Respect my wishes." He yearned to reach out to her and soothe her pain because he knew the loss of a loved one too well, and she had lost her sister. But he couldn't get in the middle of this conflict.

"It is the right thing to do, Gina. Forgive her. At least talk to Toni. Please."

Gina scoffed. "Was it the right thing to do when she betrayed me? Was it right then?"

Stephen switched off, his shoulders tensing as he abruptly got up. "I am sorry, but I need to leave. I have an appointment."

Gina nodded. "Fine. I'll walk you out." She opened the front door and slammed it behind her.

Stephen turned around. "I will see you tomorrow."

She shook her head with her hands on her hips. "Is that all you can say? See you tomorrow? Why didn't you defend me in there? I needed your support."

Stephen huffed. "I'm sorry, but I didn't think it was my place to get involved. I only just met your parents, which I wasn't planning on. It's between you and them."

She inched forward, her face softening. "You're right." As he moved towards his car, she grabbed him by the shoulder. "Listen, I didn't mean for you to meet my parents but I didn't know you'd be dropping by."

He nodded. "It's fine. As long as they believe we're only colleagues, we're good."

A fleeting look of disappointment flashed in her eyes. Did that bother her? "Oh, well, that is good, I suppose. I'll see you later." He reached for her and kissed her on the lips, but she pulled away.

He swallowed. "Are you all right?"

She squeezed his shoulder. "All good." She averted her eyes.

He forced a smile.

Stephen hated how his shoulders felt like they were weighing him down, and how the back of his neck sweated. Was she mad at him for not wanting to be official with her parents? She couldn't possibly expect more than casual as he couldn't offer her more than that. "You'd better not leave your parents waiting."

Gina stood near his car. "I'll see you soon."

Stephen shut the door and sped off after she headed back inside without a second glance. Why did he get the impression she was mad at him, or was it only his imagination?

Gina waved goodbye to her parents when her laptop, which sat on the coffee table, resounded with a Skype call. She lay it on her lap as she sat back against the couch. "Hi, Rose. Great to see you."

Her friend's easy-going hazel eyes stared at her with curiosity as she flicked her long, strawberry blonde fringe away from her cheek. She looked beautiful. "Gina, my lovely. How are you doing?"

"Great," she lied. "Tuscany agrees with you." The backdrop of rugged mountains through huge bay windows made her envious. "Gianni's house looks amazing. I wish I was there with you."

Rose nodded. "I must say, it's spacious—and it's my home now. You could fit a few families in here, but I love it."

"I can see that. How's the guesthouse doing? Do you have many guests?"

Rose's eyes lit up. "We have a waiting list now, and a few of them are students from when I last taught in Montepulciano. As of this minute, we have a maximum capacity of ten guests."

"I know you have four bedrooms, so are the guests families or couples?"

She nodded. "A bit of both, so it's nice and cosy. But ten is the right amount to manage, given the space on the minibus."

"How's Gianni, your dream man?"

Rose chuckled. "He is working at the moment, but he'll be home soon." She leaned in. "Now, enough about me. How is Stephen?

She shrugged. "Fine. We're working hard building his businesses, and he accidentally met my parents."

Rose's eyes widened. "What? How did that go?"

Gina cowered a little. "He panicked, as he didn't want to meet them, but they think he's my client and nothing more."

Rose sighed and scratched her shoulder. "Why didn't you tell them he's your boyfriend?"

Gina's hands shook. "It wasn't the right time to tell them. Besides, they might not take him seriously, Rose."

"What do you mean?"

She briefly closed her eyes, hating how deep her feelings were for the man. "I don't know if we're going to last. He can be intense sometimes, and then other times, he's playful and fun. He's helped me relax a little and not worry so much about things, but I don't know if I'm ready for more, Rose. I don't know if he's even the commitment type of guy."

Rose nodded. "It sounds like you're the one scared of commitment. Worried he's going to hurt you in the long run. Is that it?"

"I don't know. There are no guarantees in life. Look at my ex, Steven. He was my dream man and made me feel alive, but, that was all a lie. When he realised I wanted to get serious, he...well, you know what he did."

"Not all men are going to leave, Rose. Give Stephen a chance. He might surprise you. I think this issue with Toni might be impacting your relationship with Stephen. It's out there, bothering you. She's family and you need to at least communicate with her. How long has it been?"

Gina's heart ached. She missed her sister and how close they had been before she betrayed her. "At least three years now since we spoke, but it's hard. She did the wrong thing, and I still can't get past it."

Rose's eyes softened. "I hear you. Fear. That's what it is. Fear of opening up to that pain with your sister again, and fear of falling in love with a man who is the opposite of you."

How could she fall for Stephen when he only wanted casual? He'd only hurt her in the end. She was sure of it.

CHAPTER 30

Gina sat at the high table and held a glass of Lambrusco as her eyes darted around the nightclub in search of Stephen. Dalia and Teresa watched her with concern as they sipped their vodka drinks. *Where is he?*

"Are you sure you told him you were coming here tonight?" Dalia asked.

She nodded. "Yes. He explained how he needed to sort out an issue with one of his security guards and that he'd meet me here afterwards." It had been a week since he had met her parents, and she wondered if he'd run scared.

Teresa gave her a reassuring smile. "I am sure he'll be here. Don't worry so much."

"He's almost an hour late. I know he's not the most punctual person but something's wrong," Gina said.

"Ask the bartender where he might be. He might've called in," said Teresa.

"No, let's enjoy our drinks and not worry. I am done worrying all the time," she said. Gina had noticed how, in the workplace, he had been distant, but she might have been too. She wasn't sure where this relationship was going, if anywhere.

"I am sure he's not worried about seeing your parents," said Teresa, and squeezed her hand.

Dalia leaned in as she pulled her dress down. "Help me understand, Gina. Why did you tell your parents he's only a colleague and nothing more?"

Gina's hand gripped the glass, the coldness of it soothing. "I don't know. Do you honestly believe he's serious about this, about us? He's in these kinds of surroundings and I start to think he might cheat on me. Too many temptations. He's an attractive man. How can he avoid these temptations?"

"He is loyal to you, Gina," said Dalia.

"I may not be special in his eyes when he attracts a lot of women. He has choices, and now he's late for our date." She pushed aside the ache in her heart. "I'm starting to think he's pulling away."

Teresa rose and inched forward, wrapping her arms around Gina. "Oh, love. Don't be afraid to tell him how you feel. It's best to be honest."

Gina nodded. "Is it? He might run for the hills, Teresa. You've seen him at work and how he's flirted with Jeanie. They were together before. I can't compete with a woman who's that beautiful."

"He has not flirted with her," said Teresa. "It's what you want to see, but he made it clear to her that it's over between them. Believe that."

Gina's sat up straight when Stephen walked towards them on unsteady legs. Despite looking a little tipsy, he still made her heart soar.

Stephen inched forward and kissed her hungrily on the lips. "Oh, you look good enough to eat, Gina."

She pulled away after his hands travelled around her neck, caressing. "Stop it. We have company. And you're late. An hour late."

Stephen stood by her side and wrapped an arm around her waist while nodding to her friends. "Hello, ladies. Sorry I am late, but this security guard didn't take it well when I fired him. It took a few people to throw him out the door."

Gina gazed at her man, but so far he had barely looked her in the eye after she pulled away, instead focussing on a group of beautiful women who had walked past. One of them had long blonde hair with breasts hanging out of her tight, red dress. She shifted towards him.

"Hey, Stephen. How about a dance?"

He smiled and grabbed her hand. "Perhaps another time."

The woman winked. "Until next time."

Gina ground her teeth, and her muscles quivered. Heat flushed through her body, and she wanted to punch the man when his open flirtation stared her in the face. "Was she another one you slept with?"

He squared his shoulders and took a step back. "Of course not. Why would you think that?"

She ignored the wide-eyed stares of Teresa and Dalia. "The way you were flirting with her. You gave the woman a bit too much hope, don't you think?"

Stephen scoffed. "Listen, it's part of the job. I have to be friendly, and no, I wasn't flirting. I was being a great host as it's my nightclub. I want people to feel welcome and return in the future. It's business."

"Right. Business when you grab her hand like there's hope. Do you..."

"Do I what?"

She wanted to ask whether he respected her and their relationship, but she started to wonder if she could trust him. The way he had been all over that woman made her sick.

"I don't think it's right, you being like that with that woman. I didn't appreciate it, Stephen."

"Let's talk about this another time. I don't have time for this, okay? I have a business to run and people to schmooze. Yes, schmooze as, like I said, it's only business. I thought you would understand how my business is about people, and not as much about numbers, statistics, and facts. That's your department."

Gina's breath stopped. Was that a criticism? "Are you saying I am not a people-person? Is that what you're implying?"

His body stiffened and he pressed his lips together. "It's not what I'm saying. I am only saying that you see negativity in everything and think I was flirting when I wasn't. I love people, so don't try to change that about me. You accept me as I am or not at all."

Gina rubbed the back of her neck, and her stomach churned. Her accelerated breathing made her dizzy as if the room was spinning. She took calming breaths as Stephen walked to another group of women. Was that Jeanie?

"Hi, Gina. Fancy seeing you here," said Jeanie, whose scrutinising stare told her she wasn't welcome.

"Hello, Jeanie."

The other woman nodded to Teresa. "Hello there."

"Jeanie," Teresa said. She pointed to her companion. "This is Dalia."

Dalia intervened. "Hi, Jeanie. Pleased to meet you."

Stephen approached his girlfriend. "How about a dance?"

Gina shook her head. "No, I'm fine. Not in the mood." Her heartache and tight chest made her rage inside. The best thing was for her to leave and get space away from this man who thought flirting with other women was okay. How could she trust someone like that?

"I'll dance with you, Stephen. Like old times," Jeanie said. He remained silent and turned to Gina with a neutral expression.

A tingle in Gina's legs made her sway as she glanced at her hands, hoping he wouldn't play Jeanie's game. But she wouldn't give him the satisfaction of showing that she cared right this minute. "Schmoozing is part of the job, isn't it?"

Stephen turned to Jeanie. "You know what? Why not? Let's dance, Jeanie. Like old times." He put an arm around her waist and walked off with Jeanie and her friends without looking back.

Spots flashed in Gina's vision and her heartbeat slowed, her surroundings becoming surreal. A gentle hand on her shoulder jerked her back in her seat.

"Are you all right?" Teresa asked.

Gina nodded. "All good."

Dalia scrutinised her and rose from her seat to stand beside her. "I'm sorry. He was being a right jerk, but he was just angry, and it's only a dance. He cares about you, Gina. I can see how much he cares. He's tipsy too."

"I could have handled it better, I know, but he made me furious. I don't think he cares about me, Dalia. Not one bit." She rubbed a lone tear running down her cheek. "I have to go. I can't stay here and watch him...with her."

"We will go with you," said Teresa. "We can have a nice cup of tea at my house."

Gina shook her head. "No, I'd rather go home. But thanks for your support."

She walked beside them with heavy legs, struggling to breathe into her constricted lungs. No, she was making this bigger than it was. Tomorrow things would look different, and she knew that if it didn't work out with Stephen, she would survive as she always had. But why did her heart feel like it would explode right out of her chest?

CHAPTER 31

G ina pulled the drapes closed as she slouched her way over to bed two nights later. Snatching away the pillows, she threw them behind her onto the plush carpet, not caring about the mess when her mind was still reeling from the pain in her chest and image in her mind. The vision of Stephen walking off with Jeanie to God knows where, to do God knows what. No, she wouldn't think about that. Surely, he wouldn't cheat on her when they hadn't broken up—or had they? Was this his way of telling her it was over between them?

She lifted the soft grey comforter and quilt and fell into bed, the ache in her chest causing her to lose breath. Why had she left when she should have stayed at the nightclub and talk it through with him? She had allowed him to dance with Jeanie in an effort to show she didn't care, but she did. Her reaction had been out of control, and in that moment, she had needed space to think and not feel. Part of her wanted him to choose to stay with her, but instead, he had decided to walk off with Jeanie without caring how it had affected her. Well, it had, and he should have stayed by her side.

But what if she had sabotaged the relationship and made him fall easily into Jeanie's arms? What if Stephen cheating on her was all her doing?

She hadn't spoken to him since that night, and he hadn't called or visited. Were they done or were they only giving each other space? Surely, they couldn't leave it this way when nothing had been resolved. Besides, he'd had a bit to drink and hadn't been clear-headed.

As she lay in bed she looked at her phone on the bedside cabinet. What if she called him to apologise? He might be at home resting or watching TV. But what if he had cheated on her?

Stephen gripped the steering wheel as he headed to Gina's house in Coburg. He had worked late at the office and couldn't leave earlier than nine-thirty. His heart ached at having not spoken to Gina for two days, so he'd decided to talk and sort things out. He could barely remember what he had said or done.

He stopped at a traffic light on Sydney Road as his mind turned back to the night at the club when he'd headed off with Jeanie, leaving Gina with her friends. Flashing back, he remembered:

His headache worsened as he downed shots with Jeanie and her friend. They had finished dancing when she wrapped her arms around his shoulders and leaned in towards his lips, about to kiss him. But he had pulled back and pushed her away.

She had stared. "Come on, Stephen. Remember the great times we had? How I made you orgasm twice in one night? I can pleasure you again. Just one night."

He had made the wrong decision by dancing with Jeanie when he was meant to be with Gina. But he had been angry that she didn't seem to care whether he stayed with her or not. He had needed to teach her a lesson. It was immature and childish; two traits she no doubt would have agreed that he had.

He had started feeling dizzy and moved to the couch, pushing two fingers against his temple when Jeanie sat on his lap and straddled him. Pushing her off, he attempted to stand but his head throbbed like nothing else. Why did he have to drink himself into near oblivion?

"Come on, Stephen. Why don't you and I go back to your place? I'm sure you're not getting the same kind of pleasure from Gina. She abandoned you, didn't care if we got together. Doesn't that tell you something? She doesn't give two shits about you."

He thought about how Gina would possibly be leaving for Queensland to start her new business and how they'd no longer be together, even casually. Why not have fun with Jeanie? She knew how to excite him, and he could forget about Gina. He couldn't offer her more than friends with benefits anyway, and he couldn't fall for her when his heart would break all over again. He had to protect himself.

Jeanie touched him on the shoulder. "Let's go, honey."

He pushed aside his guilt. "All right. Lead the way." Walking alongside Jeanie, he bowed his head thinking that having sex with another woman would help him breathe again. No pressure and no expectations.

Now, Stephen turned off the motor and stepped out of his car. He walked across the nature strip and down the brick paved path towards Gina's front door. He rang the doorbell in the hope she'd still be awake at ten o'clock.

She opened the door, wearing a nightgown. "It's late, Stephen. What are you doing here?"

"Can I come in?" She swung the door wide open and ushered him inside.

He sat on the couch and rested against the pillow with one leg crossed over another while Gina sat at the other end. "I wanted to apologise for the other night. I had a bit too much to drink and wasn't in my right mind."

She exhaled. "Why would you go off with Jeanie?"

He flashed back to that night when he'd almost had sex with Jeanie. He was a fool and had been too drunk to think clearly. He had been hurting. But luckily, when he'd reached her front door, he'd backed away. He'd caught an Uber and left before he did anything stupid. He couldn't cheat on Gina. It wasn't who he was. "I shouldn't have done that, but I was drunk." His eyes scanned the room and came to rest on the photo of her, her parents, and her sister on the TV unit. She looked happy then. No doubt before the troubles had occurred with her baby and ex-boyfriend. "Like I said, Jeanie and I had a brief history, but it didn't mean anything."

"Did something happen between you two the other night?"

He angled his head and hated that she didn't trust him. "What? Of course not."

Gina stood up and paced across the rug, then stepped onto the floorboards and drew open the curtain slightly to stare through the window into the darkness. "You had your arms around her, and she was all over you. She's a beautiful woman. You can't tell me you weren't tempted."

Stephen walked towards her, not wanting to speak to her back. He wasn't the type to lie. "I might have been tempted but I backed out. I would never cheat on you, Gina. Yes, she is beautiful, and she might've tried to kiss me at the club, but I pushed her away." Gina said nothing. "Please say something."

She turned but stood cross-armed. "Right. You were tempted? Great. Just great. I should have known that all men are the same. Can't keep their penises in their pants. Why would you be any different?"

"I didn't do anything, Gina."

She shook her head, pushing back a tear. "No, but you cheated in your mind, and you had every intention of sleeping with her." Stephen was a jerk, but maybe he didn't know how not to be. "Do you still believe you have to flirt with women for business? Isn't that what you said? That you need to schmooze women for business?"

"I have to be friendly, yes, and flirt innocently, but nothing more." Stephen put his hands back into his pockets. "There is nothing wrong with harmless flirtation. It's business and not personal. I can't help it if women throw themselves at me. It's their issue, not mine."

Gina nodded. "Right. But you were tempted by Jeanie?"

He shook his head. "Yes, but only because... I don't know why. I was angry with you for acting like you didn't care whether I stayed or not. But I'm a people person and women are my main customers at the club, so you need to accept that it's a part of my business to be friendly with women." Stephen knit his brows and headed towards her, but she waved him away. "Why are you still angry? I told you I didn't cheat. I wanted to get that straight and not make you believe I was a cheater. I'm not. I've never cheated on a woman I've been committed to."

"I am angry because you think it's okay to flirt with other women for the sake of business. I am angry because you entertained the idea of sex with Jeanie. I am angry because you flirted with her at the club. You didn't even initially tell me the truth about your history with her." She scoffed. "I don't know if I can trust you with women who throw themselves at you because you don't bother to inform them that you're taken. You give them hope, and I can't tolerate that when I've had an ex-partner cheat on me. I was a challenge for you, another notch on your belt. How can I trust that you won't be tempted by another beautiful woman like Jeanie again?" She swallowed. "These women throw themselves at you and you act as if it's okay. I'm not fine with it, and if you expect me to be, then what are we doing in a relationship? My ex-partner claimed he would never cheat, but that didn't happen, did it?"

Stephen shook his head. "Please do not put me in the same basket as your ex. Like I said, I am not the cheating type and never was." He took a calming breath despite clenching his hands. "Besides, aren't you planning to relocate to Queensland? Something you failed to mention to me. Do you expect us to still see each other then?"

She averted her eyes. "I don't know, but it's obvious you're not committed. Especially when you met my parents. As soon as you got there, you wanted to run for the hills."

"I never gave you any expectations about us. We're friends with benefits and we enjoy each other's company. Isn't that enough?"

He couldn't fall for Gina when she'd most likely leave and break his heart. It was better to resume his flings with women without having to lose what he never had. He wasn't ready to lose Gina, but he couldn't offer her much more than he already had.

CHAPTER 32

S tephen huffed. "I think you're looking for any excuse to find problems where there aren't any. Do you genuinely not trust me?" Silence. "Gina?"

She shrugged. "I don't know if I can after the other night. Over the last few months, I've seen Jeanie flirt with you; she obviously still likes you. But as I said, you couldn't be bothered to tell me you had been together until the last minute. Trust needs to be earned."

He sighed. "If you don't trust me, then what is this? What are we doing here in a so-called relationship? You didn't seem to care whether I went off with her at the club or not, so don't wholeheartedly put the blame on me, Gina."

"I can't talk about this anymore."

His eyes hardened. "No, we still need to talk." He shook his head. "You knew who I was when we made love and started a relationship. You knew about my businesses and the type of person I was. I don't appreciate you trying to change who I am. Being rude to women you barely know when I have a reputation to uphold. Always looking at the negative side of things while barely ever relaxing or letting go of yourself. When I wanted to help you with your paintings, you bit my head off. You're scared of putting yourself out there, of living life, and you love to complain about every little thing. Now I'm the bad guy."

"I don't appreciate you trying to change *me*. I am who I am, and I want to get my paintings out there when I'm ready. It's something I need to achieve on my own, and like I said, I am my own woman, Stephen." She exhaled. "Why did you give me that special night at the masquerade party? Was that for the sake of repeat business?"

His chest tightened. "What a joke. Do you think our relationship has been a lie when I've always treated you with respect?"

"Where do you see this relationship going?"

He shrugged. "I don't know. But it's obvious we're too different to make it work. I can't cope with your judgements, your negativity, your need to be so damn uptight all the time. You need to let go and trust sometimes. It's as if you love being miserable."

"And you are so damn self-centred and unrestrained that I can't trust you won't be tempted by a woman one of these days. It's who you are, and I can't change who you are, can I? I don't need another Peter Pan in my life."

His vision blurred, and the gut-wrenching pain made him unsteady on his feet. "And I don't need someone who's wound so tight she thinks that being impulsive and optimistic is a crime. Someone who complains about everything and everyone. Who doesn't seem to believe in a mature adult relationship with trust. Perhaps you're right. I do need someone who accepts me for who I am, and you only want me to be who I'm not."

"No doubt about that. A part of me always knew we wouldn't last. You had your fun—your conquest—and so did I, but I don't think we can work when there's no trust."

He gasped, unable to believe she saw him that way when he cared about her. Still did. He couldn't tell her because his body was boiling. Tears fell down her cheeks.

"I already explained that I can't offer you anything more. This is it."

"Right. I know you need someone different. Someone who isn't so negative or loves to be miserable. Isn't that what you said?"

His heart ached, but he couldn't make her understand him. Stephen felt a chill up his spine. His legs felt heavy, and his chest ached. Even his hands trembled. "Are you breaking up with me?"

Gina looked down at the ground. "Yes. If I can't trust you, then we're living a lie." She shed another tear. "We're done."

"If that's what you want. Fine."

"Great," she said.

He looked away, opened the door and rushed out towards his car without looking back. Stephen drove for five minutes before stopping and pulling over to the curb. He bowed over the steering wheel, punched into it, then sat in silence, with a big gaping hole in his chest. He was better off with his flings. Less painful that way.

CHAPTER 33

The next day, Gina threw a t-shirt inside her suitcase. Dalia stood beside her and shook her head, staring at her with concern.

She wiped away her tears, squared her shoulders, and zipped up the bag, then stared hard towards the open window of her bedroom. What was she doing? Running away? Needing to get away from all that was familiar?

Dalia threaded a hand through her hair. "Why not talk to Stephen when you've had time to calm down. You were both angry last night and need to process things. I know he cares, and he confirmed he didn't cheat on you."

Gina pushed aside her gut-wrenching pain, a part of her knowing that she needed to communicate with the man, but it was too much. The past wound around her neck like a noose she needed to untie. The suffocation was too much when she thought about her other losses: her unborn daughter, Steven, her sister. The grief was intolerable, and she needed a change of scenery to escape and get her emotions under control. It was the right thing to do. "Stephen was a mistake, Dalia. He's got too many temptations when he chooses to flirt with women as if he doesn't have a woman waiting for him at home. I can't handle his flirtations. Whether he cheated on me or not, it doesn't mean he never will. Being tempted by Jeanie only tells me how weak he is. That he'd betray me like my ex did."

"You need to let go of the past so you can learn to trust Stephen." Dalia gave her a reassuring smile. "The past is clouding your judgement, Gina. Without trust, it would never work. But I know you love him. Isn't he worth fighting for?"

She struggled against her shortness of breath. "I need to get away. I called my boss and asked for a few days off, and hopefully by then, I'll get over him." She crossed her arms then sat on the edge of the bed while Dalia put an arm over her shoulder, giving her a reassuring smile. "I love him, Dalia. I know that now, which is why it hurts so much, and I will break down if I see him. I can't go through that pain again. Talking won't achieve anything."

"Take some time. You can't make big decisions when you're feeling vulnerable."

Gina headed over to her phone which was ringing on her bedside table, and checked the display. It was an unknown number. Her shoulders drooped. Did a part of her want it to be Stephen calling her? "It's no-one."

"I was stupid to fall in love with the man and think he could have been different. I'm done with men. Done with romance. It's too much." He never once told her how he felt about her, and she was starting to think she had only been a challenge to him. Nothing more. The man was out of her league, and she'd always be wondering whether he would cheat on her.

Gina headed back to the couch and sat down, massaging her hands.

Stephen walked past his receptionist, Julie, on Tuesday morning. "Send me the resume of my ten o'clock interview. I seem to have lost it."

His receptionist nodded. "Of course. Right away."

A few of his staff members waved in his direction, but he brushed them off and looked away. He wasn't in the mood to be friendly.

He stormed into his office with clenched fists, a fire burning in his chest and his body tired from lack of sleep last night. He couldn't get Gina out of his mind, and yet he couldn't control his fury at the world and at the woman he cared about.

Booting up his computer, he scrolled down to his emails and clicked on the resume of his applicant for the new Osteopath position at the Mount Macedon Centre. She was highly skilled and had vast experience. He had a few other interviews later today, but his mind wouldn't be on any of them. His mind kept flitting from Gina and the way she made him feel to the way she had discarded him like a piece of rubbish.

Did she not realise how deeply he cared and wanted to see her every minute of the day? But they were done, at least for now. It was for the best. As far as he was concerned, he couldn't see her again until his rage simmered down.

Stephen rose and stared through the window at the city skyline, compressed buildings, traffic congestion, and passersby walking along as if they didn't have a care in the world. He struggled to focus on work. He couldn't get the pain in her eyes out of his head when he had criticised her uptight ways. It had been hurtful and unwarranted, but he'd been raging at the time, and she had dictated how he should behave. He couldn't cope with her leaving him for her new business, losing her to sickness, or her finding another man. Either way, she'd leave him in the end. But damn, his heart felt broken and empty, as if he'd lost one of his arms. He was stuck in his pain and couldn't even disclose that his feelings for Gina ran deeper than he was willing to admit.

A knock on the door broke him out of his reverie. "Come in."

Dale stepped inside and sat opposite Stephen with a raised brow. He looked at his friend with a shake of the head. "What is going on with you, Stephen? You've been barking at everyone and being rude to Jeanie. What's going on?"

"Nothing. I am preoccupied with these interviews for osteopaths today. If you'd like to sit in, you're welcome."

Dale rested back against the chair and flung his right leg over his left. "Sure, but you still haven't answered my question, man. Don't tell me it's nothing. I know you, man. What the hell's wrong with you? You're usually so excited and playful with everyone, but this morning you've been dark and moody."

Stephen moved away from the window and sat down, picking up a pen and flicking it between two of his fingers. "Gina and I broke up."

Dale's eyes widened and he winced. "Are you serious?" He nodded. "What the hell happened? You two were tighter than my running shoes."

Stephen explained their fight. "She hates me and doesn't accept me for me." He waited for his friend to say something but the look on his face told him everything. "Are you judging me now too?"

Dale shook his head. "No, I'm not. I love you, man, just as you are, but when it comes to women, you are so damn stupid."

"Right. Hit me where it most hurts."

"If you took a minute to see it from her perspective, you do flirt with women and act as if you're still single. Were you trying to push her away on purpose by thinking you could sleep with Jeanie?"

Stephen swallowed. "Of course not." But had he been? Did he want to sabotage his relationship by thinking of having sex with Jeanie?

"I think you were trying to drive her away because you're scared, man. Admit it."

"Ridiculous. I am pain-free."

"Admit that you love her more realist nature and I'm sure she'll forgive you."

"I still don't think I need to justify the way I am to her. It is good business to be friendly with my customers at the nightclub. I'm a friendly and open guy. Nothing wrong with that."

"She is not Katie, man. Gina's healthy and she cares about you."

He explained her possible relocation. "Even if we were together, she'd eventually leave for Queensland. Either way, they all leave in the end, Dale."

"Talk to her. If she knows how you feel, you guys can work it out. Give it a chance before you think of the worst scenario."

He checked his watch. "I'm done with this conversation, Dale. I have to prepare for this interview and have a load of other things to do. Meet me back here before ten."

Dale stood up. "Fine, but you need a reality check, man. I say, if Gina's the one, do not pass on the opportunity to be in a relationship with the woman you love."

His heart skipped a beat. "Who said anything about love?" But then again, he couldn't eat, couldn't drink, couldn't focus, and dreamed about her every day and night. Was he in love with her without realising it? Had he been from the beginning?

CHAPTER 34

Gina sat on a weathered timber bench, gazing out over the thick tree trunks with their sprouting branches above the river, calm ripples, and sunlight casting shadows over the water. Smells of lemon, perfume of the spring wattle, and images of bronzewing pigeons gave her comfort.

She had loved waking up in the early morning mist as she crunched her feet over scattering leaves of assorted colour. In the night, she had snuggled up in her blankets in bed to hear birdsong and croaking frogs. Now in the late afternoon, she felt the sunlight warming her face, which helped her to forget her problems.

She had needed this bed-and-breakfast get-away in the Yarra Ranges to think about her life and what she had to look forward to. How could she keep working with Stephen when she knew she'd never again get to kiss those tasty lips, feel his hands caress the small of her back or make love to him in a warm bed? How could she avoid this deep ache in her heart and emptiness in her soul, living without the man she so desperately loved? But he obviously didn't feel the same way about her when he hadn't told her once how he felt. The burn in her chest and chills in her fingers made her want to cower and crawl under a rock.

The snap of a twig alerted her to footsteps behind her, a flash of Stephen in her mind. But the noise came from another set of guests. A couple who waved, walked off and kissed each other while taking a morning stroll. For a second there, she had hoped it was Stephen coming to rescue her from her pain. But he didn't know where she was, and she had Teresa filling in for her. Besides, he wouldn't drive all the way here with his busy schedule.

She rose from the bench, and walked back to her room, admiring the low brush, array of flowers, and trees among beds that surrounded the quaint cottage house. A white fence wrapped around the building in front of the backdrop of mountains and a cluster of trees. She stepped over freshly cut lawn and made her way up the steps and inside her room.

Sitting back against her bed, she picked up a romance book and flicked to her bookmarked page. Why not live vicariously through someone else's romance ordeals?

But her eyes couldn't stay open on the page when Stephen's handsome face stayed at the forefront of her mind. When she missed him after not seeing him for almost two days. The pain in her head and quiver of her body made her want to forget him. For her own sanity, she had to.

When her laptop pinged with a video call, she half-hoped it was Stephen. She rushed over to it on the desk beside the bed and opened it up. "Hi, Rose. Isn't it about eight in the morning there?"

"It sure is, darl. No rest for the wicked. Where are you? It looks pretty."

Gina didn't want to explain what was going on. "I've taken a few days to get some country air. A bit of a break."

Rose flinched and pointed to her. "You? Taking a break from work? Who are you and what have you done with Gina?"

Gina deflated as tears misted in her eyes. "Oh, Rose."

"Darling, what happened? Talk to me."

After rubbing her eyes, she explained the whole story and waited.

"Oh, that's terrible you guys broke up. I thought you were tight. Can't you talk to him when you're both not so angry? Hurting each other is not good karma, and you both need to work together."

"I know, but we're done. Broken up. There's no fixing this, Rose. He chooses to be an arsehole by flirting with women, thinking it's okay, and I get to be the uptight bitch he can't stand. The one who loves misery."

"That's bullshit. You guys complement each other, and the best way to move on from this is to be true and honest. You love each other, so it's worth the fight. Don't let one argument finish it."

"He doesn't love me, Rose."

"How do you know that?"

She shrugged. "I just know. Besides, if he truly loved me, he wouldn't think that flirting was okay, or he would've fought harder for us."

"But you were angry at the time. He might need a little time to process, but don't give up on him just yet. Look at Gianni and me. We made it work because our love made it worth the sacrifices."

"I don't know. I can't trust the guy, so what kind of foundation is that for a relationship? I don't want to wonder about whether he's sleeping with someone every time he's working at the nightclub. He has too many temptations."

"Maybe so, but if he loves you, he wouldn't be tempted. Talk to the guy or I'll have to talk to him on your behalf."

"I don't know, Rose." Gina wondered whether they could at least get closure, even if they weren't meant to be together. "Let's talk about you, Rose. How's life in Montepulciano?"

As she listened to Rose rant on about a funny guest, she laughed at the way her friend brought her much-needed joy. She had always known how to cheer her up and loved her like a sister. She no longer had a sister, but at least she had her friends.

CHAPTER 35

G ina avoided Stephen's eyes as she pointed to the screen. "We have the baseline numbers, and here we hope to have the conversion numbers or projections for the advertising Teresa plans to implement." She took deep breaths and continued to avoid looking at Stephen. Instead, she focused on his usual team but wondered where Jeanie was. It was a relief not to see that woman continue to flirt with him.

Gina had spent a restful few days at the bed-and-breakfast and felt refreshed but was still hurting. Stephen had not once attempted to call her. What was the point when they were over before it had truly begun?

"What are your ad strategies for the Mount Macedon centre?" asked Dale.

Gina exhaled and put down documents while pointing again at the projected screen. "Search engine optimisation on the site with a fresh landing page that offers a reader magnet about health education. We'll be doing Google search advertising. A website expert on our team will improve the speed with a better user experience, including pop-ups, adding richer keywords and a speedier search function. Overall, a better website experience. Not to mention A/B testing to see what works." She locked eyes with Stephen before turning away. "We believe that creating another health hub for Mount Macedon can help us target acute health issues and chronic conditions. Therefore, have an improved website speed, location search functions, and overall website navigation."

Stephen raised his hand. "What about the New Zealand centre? Any ideas about our next steps?"

Gina huffed. "If you'd been listening, I explained how our other creative team will take that on. Teresa and I can only do so much. Unless you'd rather we didn't eat or sleep, then sure, we can do it."

Stephen glared. "I am not suggesting that at all, but you might have mentioned it in passing because *I* did not hear you."

"Of course you didn't because you think that life is a bed of roses. If we have enough positive energy, we can conquer the world. You live in a dreamworld."

Stephen got up and placed his hands on his hips. "Since when does me asking about New Zealand venture into a discussion about dreamworlds? I have the right to ask about my businesses, and I don't need you to humiliate me in front of my team."

Gina squinted. "You should find someone else you can control and leave me out of all your damn businesses." She picked up her documents and satchel and raced out of the room before she crumbled.

Heading to the exit, she ran to her car and got in. Texting Teresa, she explained how she'd wait for her outside. What had she done? Humiliated Stephen and herself because she'd been emotional? It wasn't good business, and now he'd hate her with a vengeance.

When Teresa entered the car, she leaned in and hugged her friend. "Oh, Gina. I am so sorry about you and Stephen." She pulled away. "It's obvious that you're struggling to work with him so let me take over. You can work on our other waiting projects."

Gina nodded. "I would appreciate that, but I can do this. I can do a lot of it virtually, so I don't have to see him again."

"He is being a creep, and you don't deserve that, but you're both very angry right now. Perhaps more time apart will do you both good. But are you sure you can't have a deep heart-to-heart with him? At least get closure. This is bad karma, and we want the good energy in our work.

Remember, darling, you need to take care of yourself. Go to a meditation retreat, do yoga, or go for a jog. Anything to get you out of your body and away from thinking too much. Mindfulness can work wonders."

"I just came back from the country, but I might go for a jog after we get back to the office. Do you mind if we leave early?"

"Of course not."

Gina started the motor, and a love song came on the radio, reminding her of the night they'd made love at the masquerade party. Keeping her hands on the steering wheel, the sting of tears caused her to sit frozen in time until the soft touch of her friend alerted her to the present.

"Oh, Gina. Let me drive, darling. You are in no fit state."

She shook her head, took a calming breath, and put the car into drive. "I'm good." She wondered if this aching pain would ever leave her chest.

Stephen's body froze at the way Gina rushed out of the room. Most of his team left with stricken faces except for Dianne and Rob.

Why did a rush of guilt flood his body? He felt like a jerk for reacting the way that he had. Rather than de-escalating the situation, he had made it worse.

"You're an idiot," said Dale.

He faced his friend and the shocked faces of his team. "What?"

"Did you have to be such an arsehole? You obviously didn't hear her talking in the beginning, so why be rude?"

"Gina wasn't pleasant either. It works both ways."

"You are both being childish," said Rob. "But you cannot treat women as if they're the enemy. She has her quirks, and you do too."

"Yes, I agree, but for us to make an informed decision, let's hear what started all this. I know it had something to do with Jeanie because she was crying here the other day after you got rid of her. What exactly happened?" Dianne asked.

"I would rather not get into it," said Stephen. He was tired of feeling despondent, furious, empty, and sad. He missed Gina like crazy, but she'd pushed his buttons when she humiliated him in front of his team. She was still playing games.

Dale ignored what he'd said and explained the whole story to Rob and Dianne. "So, there you have it. A man who thinks he can treat a beautiful woman that way." He turned to Stephen. "You need to appreciate Gina like a fine wine that matures with richness. We've noticed the changes in her for the better, and yet, you haven't changed. You still live in the past. You need to face the loss of Katie. Your fear is holding you back. We all die eventually, but it doesn't mean we should stop living because of it."

"Exactly," said Dianne. "If you were my boyfriend, I wouldn't trust you either after the way you walked off with Jeanie, especially knowing that she still had a thing for you. What did you expect Gina to think? She knew about your history with her, and yet, you decided to shove Jeanie in her face. Were you trying to get her to dump you before you dumped her?"

Stephen huffed. "I know when a woman doesn't care enough about me to sort things out. She talks about doing the right thing, but she treated me like dirt in front of everyone."

"Oh, get over yourself," said Rob. "Don't act all high and mighty and superior because you're not. I admit she shouldn't have bit your head off, but you should have taken her out of this room and spoken to her properly. Apologise for your behaviour and tell her how you feel. Any blind person can see you're in love with the woman. You don't see it or choose not to see it."

Was Rob right? Should he tell her how he felt? "I appreciate your opinion, guys, but I'm leaving. I need to clear my head." He scurried out of the room and outside the building.

Once he entered his car, he retrieved his phone and texted Gina. "*Can we talk?*" His heart beat fast as he waited for a reply, but he had lost all hope, so he started his engine. The buzzing sound soon lifted his spirits. Clicking on the message, his shoulders fell at the words: *Go to hell.*

Why did he bother when she wanted to play hardball? He didn't need her drama and knew he could live without her. But who was he kidding? How would he get through the rest of his days working with her when he couldn't hold her in his arms, kiss those rosy lips, or thread his hands through her glossy hair? She was stubborn yet lovable, and he loved her. How had he not realised it before, knowing he couldn't live without her? He was an idiot.

CHAPTER 36

One week after her meltdown at Stephen's workplace, Gina drove to her mother's house after being summoned. She sat outside Josephine's garden, which featured a vegetable patch, a bed of roses, and freshly mowed grass. The sunlight hit her square in the face, but she loved the warmth. The scent of freshly brewed espresso hit her nose as she took a sip of a lemon, lime and bitters, then rested her hands on the rickety table.

"How have you been, dear?" Her mother sipped an espresso then offered her an Italian biscuit.

"She shook her head. "I'm fine, Mom."

"Are you?"

"Mum, you are the one who asked me to come over. Was there a particular reason, and where's Dad?"

"Oh, he's gone to the hardware store. Had to buy a few things for the garden." She looked over her shoulder. "How is...aah...Stephen?"

Gina angled her head, curious. Why would she be asking about him when her mother never knew about their relationship? "We only work together, so why do you ask?"

Her mother waved her away. "Oh, come on, darling. When I was at your house, I could see something between you two. I'm sure that man is in love with you. He couldn't take his eyes off you, and that's when I knew. Something is going on between you two, so admit it, darling."

Gina could never fool her mother. "Sure, there was, but now we've broken up. Better that way. It would never have worked out."

Her mother bit into her biscuit. "Did he do something to upset you?"

"Oh, Mum. I'd need an entire day to explain everything, but in a nutshell, we are total opposites and would never work out. I need someone more stable, more…I don't know what I need, but relationships and I do not mix. I have had it with men." She angled her head. "But why would you think he did something wrong?"

Her mother hesitated then poured Gina a glass of water into a crystal glass. "I know you, darling. You have this strong sense of right and wrong and when something doesn't fit that mould, you judge. Sorry to say, but we all have different character traits, different opinions, or unique ways to do things which are not necessarily wrong.

If he did do something wrong, you can forgive, for not only his sake but yours too. We're human and we all make mistakes, but so long as we learn and grow from them, it's worth making those errors."

Gina knew her mother was right. "He's the type who likes to have fun. He's impulsive and sometimes doesn't think about what he does, doesn't realize that it's hurtful. He called me uptight and negative, and said that I love being miserable, but I'm a realist, Mum."

"Hmm. That you are, but have you thought you might learn something from him? Something about letting go of the past and living in the moment? Feeling free and being positive at times? Forgiveness is something we all do. That inner child beckons to come out and show the passion inside you. You're an artist, darling, and that in itself shows you are operating from a different part of the brain. Opposites do attract. Look at your father and me. We've been married for over thirty years, darling."

"But to give you context, and get your perspective, I'll explain what happened," Gina said.

Her mother placed a finger underneath her chin. "You need to make it work and talk to him, Gina. Accept that he's human, allowed to make mistakes. That he's allowed to say hurtful things to protect himself and avoid his own pain. We all do things we regret." Was her mother right?

"You mentioned his employee, Jeanie, has been fired?" Gina nodded. "Doesn't that tell you something?"

"Who knows why he fired her, Mum. It might've been for another reason." Gina knew this wasn't only about Stephen. "But he most likely fired her because she violated policy in the workplace. Sexual harassment. But what is this about, Mum? I know you invited me here for a reason."

Her mother frowned. "I don't think you believe that for a minute." She waved a hand. "But for argument's sake, if he did fire her because he cares about your feelings, then that would be a statement in itself. He cares about you more than you think. But it also sounds like he's scared of losing you like he did his late fiancée." She huffed.

"Answer me this: Do you love Stephen?"

She ignored the stabbing pain in her chest. "Yes, so much it hurts."

Gina sipped her remaining water then chatted with her mother about her latest artwork. "I am thinking about showcasing my work. There is a gallery that's in search of new artists, so I'm thinking of getting in touch."

Her mother touched her hand. "That's amazing, darling. You have such talent. Let me know when you have a showing booked, and we'll be there."

"I need to be accepted first. We'll see."

"Darling, I..." Her mother stopped talking as she peered past her.

Gina turned around and flinched. *It couldn't be, could it? After all this time?* Her sister took measured steps towards her, a dark and pained expression on her face. *Toni.* She crossed her arms. Why did her heart ache at her sister's expression? "What are you doing here?"

"Gina, I think you need the truth."

A chill spread down her spine. "What truth?"

She stared into her hands. "It's about Steven and what really happened that night."

Gina swallowed, the world seeming to be spinning around her. Why dredge this up again? Toni had betrayed her, plain and simple. "Nothing you say will change my mind. Accept that I'll never forgive you."

Her sister fixed her gaze on her after glancing briefly at her mother with a strange expression. Was more going on here?

Toni took a deep breath. "Steven drugged and assaulted me. I was so out of it when he took advantage of me. I couldn't say anything because I was ashamed of how hard I partied that night and...and...because of my addiction to drugs. I had to get help after that, but I was embarrassed by it all. I am sorry I didn't tell you sooner, Gina, but I had a lot to work out."

Gina's heart ached as she tried to process it all. She had misjudged her sister and knew in her heart she was still in pain. She stared at her sister, got up from the table, and wrapped her arms around her.

Stephen stood on his balcony and looked out at the city buildings and skyline, his arms resting atop the railing. A view of the Yarra River and natural landscape gave him little comfort as he thought about how he'd win Gina back.

He turned around, picked up his phone, and called a friend. "Listen, George, I need you to organise something for me. It has to be simple, elegant, and romantic. Money's no object, so whatever it costs, I don't care."

"Wow. Who are you trying to impress?"

"The love of my life, George. The love of my life." After making further arrangements, he ended the call with a smile on his face, his heart soaring. He was taking a risk as he didn't know if she'd accept him back. But it had been at least two weeks if not more since they'd broken up, and he missed her like he'd never missed anyone before. He knew now that he could have handled things differently and understood why he had been pushing her away. It was time to show Gina how much he truly loved her.

CHAPTER 37

Gina rubbed her hands together as she walked out of her office alongside Teresa. "I'll see you on Monday."

Teresa put up a hand. "Wait." She averted her eyes. "Listen, a few friends of mine are having a beach party at the Williamstown Beach. Why don't we go together?"

Gina shrugged. "I don't think so. I'm not in the mood to go out these days. What's the occasion?"

"Oh, it's my friend's birthday. Come on, darl. Please come. I don't want to go out on my own. I'll drive. Leave your car here and we'll pick it up later. Pretty please."

Her sense of guilt at saying no again made her change her mind. "Fine, but I'm not dressed for a party. Can I go home first and change?"

Teresa shook her head. "No time. We are dressed well, don't worry." She beamed. "Come on. Let's go."

Gina raced to catch up to her friend, who was metres ahead of her, seemingly in a rush. "Is there a deadline here?"

"Sorry, no." She walked back towards her. "Of course not." Reaching the car, Teresa took the driver's seat and Gina sat beside her, thinking it was out of character for Teresa to impulsively ask her out to a birthday party. "I am so glad you've made up with your sister."

"It was a shock to say the least. Who would've thought she was lying out of shame and because she had an addiction? She did a stint in rehabilitation but relapsed. Now, after intensive counselling, she is clean and free. I cannot believe that bastard assaulted her. I told her to report him."

Teresa turned to her. "Will she?"

"I don't know, but she's thinking about it. At least then the bastard can't hurt anyone else, but to think she kept it a secret all this time."

"It does make you wonder about how we don't truly know people or what's going on inside them. The power of forgiveness."

Gina huffed. "I know what you're doing, and it won't work. That ship between Stephen and me has sailed. Besides, if he truly cared, he would have made a move by now. Before you say anything, that text saying, 'Can we talk?' doesn't count. He should say that to my face, not through a stupid text. He obviously doesn't care about me as much as I do about him. Let's move on, shall we?" The pain in her chest told her she hadn't yet moved on.

"Okay. Fine," said Teresa.

Her friend found a parking spot. During the twenty-minute walk that followed, Gina thought about Stephen and how much she missed him. Would he fight for her one day?

She realised that she'd never given him a chance to explain why he'd been tempted by Jeanie. What had propelled him, and had Gina pushed him away without realising it? It had been the same with Toni; she'd never given her a chance to explain.

She looked at the seagulls perched across the reserve as she dug her wedged sandals into the firm grass. People sat around on picnic blankets and children played in the playground. Passing by the reserve, they crossed the road and headed to the quieter side of the beach, past the kiosk, with more people sunbathing until they reached a familiar figure in the distance.

Gina stopped in her tracks when she spotted Stephen. Her heart ached. He held a bottle of champagne next to a wine bucket on a picnic blanket spread on the sand.

She turned to Teresa. "So much for your friend's birthday party."

Teresa hugged her tight. "I'll be off now, but talk to the man. I love you. Tell me all about it later, darl." She rushed off after waving goodbye to Stephen.

Gina inched forward, her feet digging into the sand, so she took off her shoes and walked barefoot. The warmth of the sand felt nice. Tingles around her body made her yearn for his closeness, but no, he wouldn't be getting off that easy. As much as she desired to kiss and hold him, she couldn't easily forgive him. "What is this?"

Upon closer inspection, a set of plates on the blanket held cheese, crackers, bread, strawberries, and bananas. It was a feast.

Stephen ushered her over to the blanket and sat down. She joined him, sitting opposite. "I wanted to apologise, Gina. I was a bastard, and I now realise that my behaviour was childish." He raised a brow. "But only because I wasn't ready for us. I was running scared, and you thinking about relocating to Queensland, reminded me of losing Katie. I was scared I'd lose you too if we got too attached or something went wrong. But if you feel that moving to Queensland is for you, then we could make it work. You're uptight sometimes, but you're also smart, efficient, and quick at everything you do. You're responsible and hard-working, generous with your heart, lovable, gorgeous, and the way you see the reality of a situation is endearing. You're my everything. I love the way you bite your bottom lip when you're nervous or the way you tilt your head when you're confused, and even the way you brighten my spirits whenever you walk into a room. I love you, Gina, and I think I've always loved you. I was too panicked and scared to see it before, but I see it now."

"Okay," said Gina who was otherwise lost for words. Her spine became numb, and her eyes misted.

"And you were right about me flirting with other women. I should never have gone off with Jeanie and I should never flirt with other women when I am so in love with you. I can be friendly but not flirty. I know there's a fine line between the two, but I would never cross that line, Gina. I love you too much. Like I said, I've never been a cheater, not even with women I cared about less than I do about you. Don't you see? You are it for me, and I cannot breathe, sleep, or eat when you're not in my life. I not only want you in my life, but I need you. Please tell me you'll give me a second chance."

Gina took a step closer. "Those things you said were hurtful. Like you don't accept me for me. It won't work if you don't accept my flaws."

"I love that you're real and human, and I know some of that was because you were scared. You've become more relaxed about things now. I can understand why you were rude to those women at the club when you had this baggage with your ex. But please know that I am not him and never will be."

Gina knew he was not like her ex-boyfriend in any manner. She hoped he'd rot in hell after what he did to Toni. "Why did you fire Jeanie?"

"I didn't fire her. I offered for her to work at one of the country centres. She refused and ended up resigning. She knew I didn't want her close. But I did it for us. I couldn't cope with her flirting behaviour, and I was tired of pushing her away and telling her I loved you. I don't know where she is now, and I don't care. I only want you, Gina. It will always be you."

She rubbed a tear. "But how can I trust that you won't be tempted by her or any other woman next time we have a fight? You thought about sleeping with her, Stephen."

Stephen leaned in. "I was trying to push you away, finding an excuse for you to hate me and avoid getting serious. I didn't want you hurting me down the track. It was self-sabotage, but I'm ready to move forward. I was scared because of the pain over losing Katie, but now I'm willing to face my fears. I get that you only get one life, and I doubt I'll find any other woman who could even come close to you. You're it for me, and I love you so damn much, it hurts."

A tear stung her eye. "Oh, Stephen. I love you too. So much."

He inched forward and broke the gap between them. Holding her chin in his hand, he devoured her lips and stroked the small of her back. "Oh, how I love you, Gina.

"Don't ever let me go again, Stephen."

"Never," he said as he pulled her down into the sand and ravaged her with his mouth, sending her into heaven.

EPILOGUE

FOUR MONTHS LATER

G ina felt the adrenaline rush as she walked around the gallery that showcased her artwork. She carried a glass of champagne while Stephen held her hand and scrutinised the painting: the well-defined cheeks, broad mouth, soulful chestnut eyes, and shoulder-length wavy hair.

Stephen squeezed her hand, a lone tear falling down his cheek. "How can I ever repay you for painting Katie? It's like I'm seeing her all over again. Thank you." He leaned in and kissed her as if other guests weren't in the showroom. As if her parents, sister, extended family, Dalia, Teresa, and Stephen's friends weren't present.

Gina ignored the cacophony of noise around her and focussed on the man she loved. "It was a pleasure to paint her, and I'm glad you can keep her close to your heart."

He gave her a reassuring smile. "You're not jealous?"

She shook her head. "I honour your past, Stephen. She was special to you and it's okay with me."

"I've bought this one, and I'm buying the portrait of me before anyone else does."

"Right. No doubt your ex-girlfriends would want that painting, but I'd rather you bought it." She stared past him as Toni approached.

"Oh, Gina." She wrapped her arms around her. "I'm having a blast. You definitely need to paint my portrait. Pretty please?"

"Of course, Toni."

Stephen snuck away as if he was on a mission. What was going on? He approached her parents.

Teresa stood by her side. "Oh, there's going to be an announcement, Gina. Stephen has something to say." Her sister gave her a sly grin, and Gina was excited she'd moved back to Melbourne. Gina had even found a building to start her business.

Dalia linked her arm with Gina's. "Wait and see."

She nodded. "What's going on here?" No response until the love of her life walked on stage and spoke into the microphone. People gathered around and servers bustled about with trays of finger foods.

"First of all, I'd like to thank you all for coming, to honour my sexy and beautiful partner for life, Gina.

She has shown heart, dedication, love, artistic talent, and generosity of spirit in her paintings, and if some of you hadn't already bought her paintings, I would've bought the entire gallery."

"Hear, hear," said her father while her mum gave her a thumbs up.

Dale, Rob, and Dianne gazed in her direction, each with a broad grin as if they knew a secret. Would he recite strong words of love in front of everyone and embarrass her?

"Gina, I have loved you for the past six months and I couldn't imagine my life without you. Colours in my life have brightened, smells are richer, tastes are tastier, sounds are stronger, and my body feels so alive with you in it. I want to live the rest of my life with you. I want to travel with you, have babies with you, share my hopes and dreams with you. My beautiful woman. My soulmate." He reached for his back pocket and pulled open a box. Was that a ring? "Gina, will you marry me?"

She was frozen in her tracks and tears filled her eyes as the claps and shouts in the room deafened her. "What?"

"Marry me, Gina."

Dalia took the glass from her. She attempted to walk but her legs felt like jelly as Dalia nudged her over to the stage. Everything appeared surreal. Was this a dream or had the man in her life asked her to marry him?

Stephen wrapped her in his arms as soon as she reached the microphone. He pulled back. "Still waiting," he said with a devilish grin.

Rubbing the tears from her eyes, she stepped towards the microphone. "Hell yes. I will marry you."

Rounds of applause and whistles filled the room when Stephen hugged her tight and kissed her hungrily.

She was loved and safe in his arms and knew that no other man could love her like Stephen.

Reviews are GOLD to authors. If you enjoyed this book, please consider leaving a review at:

https://mybook.to/HeartsUnravelled

Check out Rose's Story in *Two Hearts And A Villa*, Book 2 of the Billionaire Romance Series below:

https://mybook.to/TwoHeartsVilla

ABOUT THE AUTHOR

Lucy Appadoo is a prolific reader and author of contemporary romance novels and the billionaire romance series alongside the Friends In Crisis and Women Of Strength Series. After a childhood spent reading and imagining escapist worlds, Lucy has put her imagination into stories.

Her work as a rehabilitation counsellor, and former work as a counsellor in private practice, have led to an interest in writing inspirational stories about authentic, driven women who manage adversity with strength and heart. She writes in the genres of contemporary romance and romantic suspense/thrillers with significant life themes.

Lucy's interests include include plotting the next love story, researching crime stories and news to inspire her work, watching crime thrillers and suspenseful movies, travel, exercising, reading for entertainment or knowledge, meditation, and spending time with friends and family. She also appreciates her Italian background and culture, which has inspired her to write imaginative stories about her parents' childhoods, leading to The Italian Family Series novels.

Check out Lucy's website and sign up for a free suspenseful book below:

https://www.lucyappadooauthor.com.au

ALSO BY LUCY APPADOO

Shadows Of The Past (Book 2):
https://books2read.com/u/3JZe1X
Secrets In The Shadows (Book 3):
https://books2read.com/u/ml88kv

Friends In Crisis Series - Romantic Suspense/Thriller

Haunted By The Past (Book 1):
https://books2read.com/u/bw2ZeY
Twisted Obsession (Book 2):
https://books2read.com/u/4DW8pk
Web Of Lies (Book 3):
https://books2read.com/u/3JXazE
Love-Obsessed (Book 4):
https://books2read.com/u/4jPKGX
Fatal Designs (Book 5):
https://books2read.com/u/3nBjy5

The Hearts Series - Romantic Suspense

Rising Hearts (Book 1):
https://books2read.com/u/mZwpoE
Forbidden Hearts (Book 2):
https://books2read.com/u/bQBKr7
Kindred Hearts (Book 3):
https://books2read.com/u/4AJKQK

Broken Hearts (prequel to Forbidden Hearts):
https://books2read.com/u/mgrnOD

Short Story Thrillers

Evening Interrupted:
https://books2read.com/u/3yZDjZ
The Dreamcatcher: https://books2read.com/u/bzaLxn
Red Flags: https://books2read.com/u/bWZ9W1
Collection of Short Story Thrillers:
https://books2read.com/u/bP5vwj

The Italian Family Series - Coming of Age Family Drama/Romance

A New Life: https://books2read.com/u/mqqwZm
The Beauty of Tears:
https://books2read.com/u/bpqwk3
Dancing in the Rain:
https://books2read.com/u/bOr7LA
A Life By Design: https://books2read.com/u/3J8ene

NON-FICTION
Grief & Loss
Moving Beyond Grief - How To Shift From Grief & Loss to Joy & Peace: https://books2read.com/u/mVNzDA
Stress Management & Anxiety

Holistic Spiritual and Mental Health - Building Resilience and Creativity by Conquering Anxiety and Managing Stress: https://books2read.com/u/47kG8A

Career Guidance

Your Holistic Career Path - Create Career Change, Satisfaction, and Work/Life Balance: https://books2read.com/u/bzYDz4

Readers' Journal

http://mybook.to/ReadersJournal

www.ingramcontent.com/pod-product-compliance
Lightning Source LLC
Chambersburg PA
CBHW020912130726
47904CB00006BA/1879